THE NEW SACRED

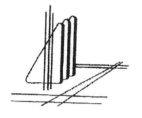

THE NEW SACRED

Measuring For Success

Don C. Davis, ThB, BA, MDiv

Archway Publishing books may be ordered through booksellers or by contacting:

Archway Publishing
1663 Liberty Drive
Bloomington, IN 47403
www.archwaypublishing.com
1-(888)-242-5904

Cover inspiration by Nolan Davis

ISBN: 978-1-4808-1646-6 (e)
ISBN: 978-1-4808-1647-3 (sc)
ISBN: 978-1-4808-1648-0 (hc)

Library of Congress Control Number: 2015935323

Print information available on the last page.

Archway Publishing rev. date: 3/10/2015

CHAPTER ONE

The New Venture

"GOOD MORNING, DR. LOGAN," STEVE SAID, WHEN DR. LOGAN answered the phone up on Eagles View Mountain, "I hope all is well up at Look Beyond cottage."

"Good morning, Steve. Yes, all is well, but very quiet up here. Good to hear from you."

Steve said, "you are always so cordial and open that I have a question. Could Sandra and I come up to meet with you a little while today?"

"Of course," Dr. Logan said immediately. "I am always pleased to have you come up here."

"Thanks," Steve replied. "Let me explain just a little. While there is never one place for an idea to originate and grow, your place up there has been a place where the dreams for the World Citizen Center began to be blended into reality. I have some ideas I would like to share which represent a new phase in that dream.

So, could you suggest a time we could come up that would align with your schedule?"

"Schedule," Dr. Logan responded in a light manner, "I have very little schedule when I am up here. That's on purpose, of course. But would around lunch time be all right for the two of you?

And, let's see now. We often have lunch when we meet up here. So, could you stop by the Home at Home Restaurant and get some lunch? No. Wait. On second thought, reverse that. I want to see if you like the kind of lunch I sometimes put together. And you don't have to imagine that I will spend a lot of time cooking this morning. In fact, the kind of lunch I create doesn't have to be cooked. It's put together.

Let me explain. As for this little lunch, because of my interest in how the brain works when we provide it with its best energy source, I have begun to focus on the foods that provide the brain with its best nourishment. Out of that interest, my mind was magnetized and drawn to a special book by a medical doctor, Dr. Neal Barnard, entitled *Power Food For The Brain*. I read it with great interest and took his advice seriously. Dr. Barnard believes that eating mostly fruits and vegetables, as our source of nourishment for the body, will also result in better energy for the brain. As for the brain part, I am not sure yet, but what I discovered almost immediately was that I felt better by eating just the kind of lunch I will prepare for us today.

Needless to say, I like the simplicity of it. Once you make this approach to food, then you really don't like the meat based menus that fast foods, and even the best restaurants, provide. Of course, there is also an environmental factor. Meat based foods have such a detrimental effect on our environment that I could almost be a vegetarian. I am not, but I like the idea, and I like the simplicity of this approach. Of course, it is not a standard for all meals, but I hope you like my little lunch. We'll see. So, just come on up. Glad to have you. It can get a bit lonely up here."

When Steve and Sandra arrived they were welcomed, and as soon as they were inside the great room, Dr. Logan said, "I don't know the full extent of what you want talk about, but maybe we could go ahead with lunch and talk about it while we eat. You are at home up here, so go on over to the refrigerator and get a bottle of water, or a little bottle of V-8, and one of those little clear plastic boxes in there that I have prepared and we can go out on the deck for lunch.

As soon as they sat down Dr. Logan asked immediately, "How's the center doing?"

"I think the center is doing fine," Steve said. "I like what Sandra says about the impact of the center. Let her sum it up."

Sandra spoke quickly and with enthusiasm. "The linkage with the church has done something great for the church. Attendance is up and membership is growing. But that is not the main measure. Having that center as an extension of our identity has energized the environment here, so every program of the church seems to have a new sense that our mission is to help all us become successful as world citizens right here in our own story."

When Sandra ended her summation, Steve continued. "We have brought in a series of great speakers. These banquets have been well attended, drawing from a wide area of people who want to keep up with the growing edge of our identity. The speakers program is an overwhelming success. But I think we have a new opportunity that I want to talk about.

We have done a lot of dreaming up here and I would like to see if we can dream some more. May I go ahead and share those dreams now?"

"By all means," Dr. Logan said eagerly. "Dreaming is what this place up here is all about. That's why I named it, *Look Beyond.*"

"First," Steve said, as though he was beginning a very well-thought out plan, "the very idea is bold, daring, and not without risks. It might not work. But on the other hand, it may just be simple enough that it will work. What we know is that we have painted our dreams with a broad brush first, then filled in details as we learn our way forward.

So, what I want to do is to go into a new phase in which we make the center into a place where we have a series of teacher training events that train and certify teachers to teach the Big Ten Universal Qualities. Then those trained teachers can go out and create their own teaching events in all kinds of settings, in small groups in their homes, in Sunday school classes, in public schools as little short term units where they are teaching. They can easily be a part of social studies, life skill classes, future scenarios, etc. - units that are never religious or political, just basic updates in defining who we can be in the greatest time ever for resetting our identity.

That's part one. Part two is that I want us to stage a series of Big Ten Success Rallies all across this region. Speakers who have read Dr. Kelly's books and tried to live out his concepts will come to speak and share how the Big Ten Universal Qualities have created new stepping stones in their own success story.

That's it in a nutshell. It is a way to expand our mission into many kinds of settings that multiply the teaching places which Dr. Kelly, called learning centers of the world. And what I envision for the success rallies is that they will be motivational events that energize people to adopt the concept of living by the Big Ten in all the places where they share their ideas and life-skills, especially in the home and family."

Steve paused a moment, then said, "As I have put these ideas together, I have put real people in my dreams. So, I just happen to have four people in mind who can bring their special skills to this dream and make it happen as a success story for themselves, and at the same time, expand what we are all about as a World Citizen Center.

Dr. Logan, you already know two of these people. They are Clark and Jenny Henderson. And I also know how much you respect and admire them. We both know they live by the Big Ten qualities in down-to-earth ways, Clark, out on the apple farm, and Jenny, in her classroom .

Two other people are equally schooled in the Big Ten. They are Brian and Linda Kelly. They are among the cousins who listened with great respect as Granddad Kelly told his stories on the farmhouse porch. Linda is a cousin by marriage to Brian, but no less a cousin, skilled and trained in working with big ideas and people, as a teacher.

But to explore this further you can ask me questions, or ask Sandra questions. She has helped me generate these dreams. She is as excited about their potential as I."

Dr. Logan was immediately engaged in the idea and didn't hide his enthusiasm. "I think you have a great idea that can have a long-term influence on helping people to rise to a higher humanity. That's at the heart of our mission as a center, to help all of us build an identity that honors the best we can be in our own future, and in the future for the human family.

So, I do have a question? Yes. How soon can we get started?"

"If we have your backing, as it has been with all we have done so far, we can get started very soon," Steve answered, with enthusiasm, mixed with caution.

"You have it!" Dr Logan said immediately. "I keep looking for great causes I can support. I can talk to the foundation board, but what I know is that they mostly leave the causes up to me, then guide my commitments so they are both noble and good business. What's the next step?"

"The next thing we need to do is to see if Clark and Jenny, and Brian and Linda buy into this idea. It could be quite a venture for them."

CHAPTER TWO

New Pioneering

BRIAN AND LINDA HAD NEVER BEEN TO THE WORLD CITIZEN CENTER, or even the unique mountain town of Alpine. Steve and Sandra had shown them a picture of the World Citizen Center once, but that in no way really described the magnificence of what they saw when they drove through the active business area, then up a winding street, and into the parking lot. Their first glimpse of the World Citizen Center after they got out of the car, caused both of them to stop and gaze in admiration as they looked up to the crest of the hill where the World Citizen Center was profiled against a background of distant mountains.

"Impressive," was the one word Brian used to describe what he was seeing.

What gave it a welcoming and personal feeling was to see Steve and Sandra standing on the patio, looking down and waiting for them to arrive. The brilliant white of the towering Three Triangles sculpture at the left, with its taller three pylons rising just in front of them, stood like a monument to the exploration of great ideas. Their magnificence made it seem like Steve and Sandra were standing at a place of distinction and importance.

The invitation Steve and Sandra had sent to Brian and Linda to come to the World Citizen Center for a visit had been cordial and welcoming, and yet mysterious, as though it were more than a visit by cousins. They were eager to find why were they being invited to the World Citizen Center instead of their home. Eagerly, they climbed the ascending walkway from the parking lot up to the distinctive center, three steps forward and one step up, three steps forward and one step up, again and again, until they were close enough that Steve and Sandra began walking down the way to meet them, with an exciting "hello" and welcoming hugs. It was the same kind of warmth they all felt as cousins when they met together at the Kelly farmhouse.

They walked up the final steps together, to where wrought iron railings bordered a long patio area, with a series of round tables and chairs. Brian lingerer a few steps behind just enough to sweep his eyes from the unique three triangles at the left, to the center, where the magnificence of the World Citizen Center was in command of its pedestal on the crest of the hill. In contrast to the ancient white of the Parthenon, the sand tone marble of the distinctive World Citizen Center was interspersed with flat faced columns only slightly darker than the marble. It truly belonged with its surrounding mountains of majestic summertime green.

Inside the large atrium, with its sequence of skylights, Brian lingered again, then stretched both hands outward as he noted, "This is impressive. Very unique! It looks like a place where any event staged here is a part of something of major significance.

"Place is important, but secondary to the dreams it is designed to advance," Steve added. "It's here we dare to think ideas that reset our identity for a far more successful future for the human family at this strategic time of unlimited potential. We are just in our beginning, but as you sense, it is a place to launch big ideas for shaping big possibilities. We invited you here, instead to our house, so you could, not only see the World Citizen Center, but feel the magnificence of the ideas we are daring to launch. Sandra and I am so pleased you are here. We want to explore some leading-edge ideas with you, but first, let's visit and catch up on our stories. Let's go into what we call the Eagles View Conference Room and sit at a table where Sandra has some refreshments waiting."

As soon as they were seated, Steve said, "We haven't seen each other in quite a while. What's been happening in your story? I have heard that both of you have completed your Master's Degree. Am I right?"

"You are right," Linda said. "Beyond that, you may know that I am a teacher, and Brian is still in the Admissions Office at the university. Not a lot has changed since we met on Granddad's farmhouse porch following his memorial service. But, Steve, what our meeting now gives me is an opportunity to express how much I appreciate that special tribute you gave to Granddad at his memorial service in the church of his boyhood, and the way you led us at the farmhouse porch and invited us to say how Granddad has influenced our lives. I think of him and Grandmother often. So, thank you for your tribute to Granddad and leading that open exploration on the farmhouse porch. I married into the family, but that didn't seem to matter, I was one of the grandchildren."

Steve responded in his usual modest manner of simple saying, "Thank you, Linda," then saying, "the influence of our esteemed Granddad continues in many special ways. In fact, this World Citizen Center is one of those special ways. It never would have been here without the influence of Granddad's dreams that he shared in his writings. So much of what we are trying to achieve here is a tribute to his legacy. Remember the Big Ten Universal Qualities? Those words are at the heart of our identity and reason for being. The opportunity to take that dream forward is the reason Sandra and I wanted to talk with both of you here. I don't want to fill in the details now, but both of you may be a part of something so simple that it may be profound.

What I want you ask you to do, as you think about this venture, is to meet two people who can bring their special skills together with yours. They are Clark and Jenny Henderson. They will be here soon."

After Steve introduced Brian and Linda, and Clark and Jenny to each other, they sat down in the Eagles View Mountain Conference Room where Steve began to explain the plan he wanted them to consider. He said, "Granddad sat on the farmhouse porch with his grandchildren, and told stories that embodied his philosophy of life and his long-reaching dreams. His dreams have become real in the World Citizen Center, but they are not finished. They have a long way to go yet. His dream was that the Big Ten Universal Qualities be taught in all the leaning centers of the world. The newest part of that dream is one we are inviting you to help make real. We propose to expand that dream through a Big Ten Teachers training program, and through Big Ten Success Rallies.

As they all shared refreshments together, Steve explained more about our the dream. He said, "In the hope that can explore all this further in a very special porch setting, I wonder, Clark and Jenny, if we could meet on the porch of your house at the apple farm. Would you consider that?" Steve asked cautiously.

"You are most cordially invited." Jenny said immediately. "We would be delighted to meet out at the apple farm."

CHAPTER THREE

Open Gates

THE DRIVE OUT TO THE APPLE FARM HELD THE SAME KIND OF AWE that it held for Steve the first time he went out to visit with Clark and Jenny. It felt like driving into adventure, as Steve and Sandra drove along the grass bordered dirt road, neatly stretching among the apple trees and both sides. Brian and Linda followed the little two-car procession in their own car. The apple farm was a place where nature's gifts had been developed to a high level of productivity to help sustain each season's supply of apples for apple pies and apple juice.

Anyone who drove out to the farm house and its nearby apply shed must have felt the welcome that Clark and Jenny gave to all who came out there. The porch, on which they were all invited to sit in its rocking chairs, had a mysterious kinship with Granddad Kelly's farmhouse porch, as though time was both doubling back and reaching forward.

Steve almost knew what the first expression of hospitality

would be from Jenny. "Would you like some sweet tea?" As only a variation, she asked, "Would you all like some apple cider?" Steve answered for all of them without asking, "Oh, yes indeed."

"Hot or cold?" Jenny's asked. I have prepared for both right over here on the table. Given the brush of autumn in the chill of the air and the blush of red on the apples, you may choose hot. Steve, which will it be for you?" Jenny asked.

"Hot," Steve said. "Matches the warmth of your welcome. Thank you so much for letting us meet out here at your delightful place."

Steve moved his rocking chair closer to the edge of the porch so he could see his little audience. "I know what I have been introducing is a big venture. I wrestled with it for a long time before I became bold enough even to share it with Sandra. After that, both of us were excited enough that I dared to share it with Dr. Logan up at his cottage on Eagles View Mountain, as a serious proposal. If you choose to become a part of this growing dream, it would involve some big changes on your part. Brian and Linda, you would need to move to Alpine. Clark, I know you would have to adjust so this fits with your apple farm. And, Jenny, you might have to align this with your teaching.

So far it's only a dream. But now we are making it into a serious proposal to the four of you. If this is something we can explore further, we can meet with Dr. Logan up at his Look Beyond cottage. As a kind of decision point, from up there you can look down and see the World Citizen Center as a vision of a mission in progress, not just to Alpine and it surrounding area, but to our human family. It's a big dream, but when we are talking about our human identity as the earth family at its time of unparalleled opportunity, big dreams are needed where there are no boundaries. A small beginning can become a leading edge for new tomorrows. I have shared the dream with Dr. Logan and he is very interested in moving it forward. We sense that this is a new call from the future and are inviting you to join us in a dream which was Dr. James Kelly's dream, that the Big Ten be taught in all the learning places of the human family. So, as you think about all this, make sure you think in terms of it being your place in a story that can be of major significance for the human family's distant tomorrows."

After explaining the program in more detail, Steve talked about the place where they would have their follow-up meeting. "Dr Logan's cottage is a very special place, unique in itself, but once you get there, you will know that a unique part of its distinction includes the groaning of the car and the scratching of its tires on a climb up and around the winding curves to get there.

We will be meeting at the mountain retreat home of Dr. David Logan, one of the truly most remarkable persons you will ever know. Just as the World Citizen Center would never have come into existence without the influence of Dr. James Kelly, likewise, the center would never have come to be without the vision of Dr. Logan, who came to World Citizen Church one day to talk to Sandra and shared his dreamed about the church having a conference center that promotes forward thinking. Dr. Logan has been, and continues to be, the energy behind the vision we are following. When we get up there we plan to meet on the deck overlooking Alpine. From there one can look down and see the World Citizen Center.

So there's a reason that the room at the center, where we met earlier, is called the Eagles View Conference Room. From there one can look up through its full glass wall and see Eagles View Mountain and Dr. Logan's Look Beyond deck. There is a dream connection between the two. Both are places where new tomorrows are envisioned as a call from the future that is in our hands, and something we can do something about by sharing our special skills.

All we are talking about is part of a knowledge-based faith, in which we need to move beyond a paradigm of transcendence, which is fading, to a paradigm of immanence, which is rising, as a world view in which our future we live in will be the one we ask for in our best dreams. We are not stuck with the hand we are dealt. We can play that hand so that we make the most of what we are given and maximize our place in a story in which the Big Ten Universal Qualities are taught in the world's centers of learning. Does that sound like Dr. Kelly? It's a dream that was at the heart of his own faith and philosophy - the one he passed on to us as the torch we can take up and carry forward."

When they got up to Eagles View Mountain, Dr. Logan had their lunch ready for them. After he had welcomed them and invited them into the great room he announced very simply. "I have a little lunch prepared for each of us. It's one that is ever so simple that even I can put it together. Sandra and Steve have tried it and they survived. This one has mixed nuts, raisins, three baby carrots, three salad tomatoes, and fruits in season like grapes, strawberries, blueberries, apples, bananas, and peaches. Today it's peaches. There is one Little Debbie fig bar and a little package of vegetable tasting crackers. There is water in a bottle, or V8, or both. To show you how formal we get up here in our dream world, each of you can just come by the refrigerator and get one of these little clear plastic boxes with its health foods ingredients, then make your way out to the deck. Once we are there, I want Steve and Sandra to introduce you further and let you tell your story. I know Clark and Jenny already, but I would like to hear more of their special story and to hear Brian and Jenny's story. We all have a story. We can share our journey stories together.

Out on the deck, Linda said, "Thank you, Dr. Logan for this lunch. Need I say that it is unusual. Delightful. Assuming there may be a connection to your philosophy of life, and that you are open to questions, I wonder if you would put it in a larger context."

"I like that," Dr Logan said. "In my mind it connects the progression in our story with the almost unbelievable earth story. I am amazed that the human family ever got through the long struggles for survival in our early history. In that long journey people would never have survived if they had not depended on killing animals for some of their food. But now that we have the wonders of scientific agriculture on a grand scale, carrying that paradigm of existence farther into our future is no longer necessary. When we go to the meat counter in our modern grocery stores, it may seem disconnected from cruelty to animals, but it's not, and no longer necessary. Scientific agriculture and bioengineering can provide us with all the nutrition we need for a healthy diet. I am not a vegetarian, but I get close. But I am an environmentalist. I believe that relying on the products of agriculture will help us to be a better environmentalist. There are many ways we can be an environmentalist. This is just one little viewpoint."

"Thanks for your candid answer to my first question," Linda said. "Do you mind if I ask another question, or two?"

"Not at all," Dr. Logan answered. "But I suggest we go inside. We are getting into the shadow of the trees now, and it's getting a bit cool as the wind is sweeping down into the valley. Steve, you know about living up here. Would you put some more wood on the fire in the fireplace, while a bathroom break is an option for all of us. Depending on Linda's question I might take a while to answer. The professor in me likes to respond to questions."

Everyone sat around the table in the great room while Dr. Logan stood with his back to the fireplace. He said, "Linda, I am eager to hear your question."

Linda spoke thoughtfully. "Dr. Logan, I get the sense that the torch Granddad passed along is one that, not only have I caught it, but you have too. It's like listening to him anew as you shared the connection of food to your philosophy of life. How do you see where we are in the long progression of the human story that has landed us in the digital-information-molecular age? And please take your time. We are not in a hurry when we hear Granddad's understandings being echoed anew. At least, I am not in a hurry."

"Nor are we," Clark Henderson said.

Dr Logan began immediately. "At MIT I teach a course in International Studies and Social Policy. It's such a broad subject that I wander far and wide. Bear with me if it seems like I am answering similar questions from my students.

As I noted, I am an environmentalist. I was immensely pleased to have Steve up here to write as an environmental scientist. The perspective I get up here is like Dr. Kelly's farmhouse porch in the sense that the quest is to define who we are in our amazing age of opportunity. But we still live in a wilderness, like John the Baptist, looking for someone to follow who would have an even larger vision of tomorrow than he had - not just resisting wrong, but leading the way to a vision of a higher right. Trying to be in step with both John, and his successor, the Teacher from Nazareth, I dream of being a part of bold new tomorrows in keeping with their idealism, updated to our digital age.

One of the great needs of our time is to live by those positive qualities which will advance humanity's story to a new level. We need so much to make our wisest choices possible, lest we only recycle yesterday and its cycle of greed, and fight-back paradigm. We are in need of models, drawn not so much from yesterday, as from dreams for new tomorrows.

While we live in the greatest age, we do not live in an ideal age. To use Dr. Kelly's metaphor, we live outside Eden, sometimes far outside, where we need to turn closed gates from yesterday into open gates to tomorrow, where we plant new gardens, where we grow new paradigms that respect the progression of science and technology, but even more, where we honor the qualities of the Big Ten. That's what the World Citizen Center is all about, and that's why I am so privileged to have a part in it!

The Big Ten contain some very important words. Caring is one of them. Collaboration is one of those words. We need to use words that help us work together with the resources we have that maximize our story which is being expanded exponentially by science and technology. In our future, robots of all kinds will do more of the work people have done for so long. But here's the big question. What about our life skills? What about learning how to live so we care about each other? We may create space flights to other worlds in our future, but what about caring and working together here, as though we have not given up on either our planet or our humanity. This is our home. This is where we not only look up and see the stars and gaze at the moon, but it's where we are creating our story as the human family with its amazing potential here in our own biosphere. It's here we are creating an environment of the minds and dreams. That environment is one we are responsible for. It's an environment which needs the humanizing effect of caring and working together in oneness.

In our modern world of human ingenuity, war is more and more primitive. If we honor the progression of our story we must get beyond our worst so we can take hold of our best. Instead of fighting against each other, we can learn to work with each other. The more we can move to a global, world citizen framework for our identity of oneness, the sooner we can honor the potential we have in our time.

What's at stake? Integrity. Nobility. Honoring the responsibility we have for creating a world that aligns with the potential of our time, that's at stake. And for that we need to dream ahead, work ahead, and teach ahead, so that Dr. Kelly's dream becomes real - that no child should ever have to say, 'I never was taught the Big Ten Universal Qualities!' That World Citizen Center down there in Alpine is your Granddad's torch still being passed along!

What's at stake? Fewer disappointments and broken dreams. Fewer people whose dreams are cut short by substance abuse. Fewer people in prison. Fewer dysfunctional families. Less poverty. Less fragmentation and more working together in our world family.

What's at stake and what's needed? An overarching faith that gives us a passion for quality based living. A quest for education and learning. A faith that aligns us with the amazing ongoing progression of science and technology and those qualities which make us world citizens wherever we are.

What's needed? An identity framework that makes children proud of their parents, and parents who are honored by their children. We need a faith that honors a larger understanding of those words, 'blessed are the peacemakers' - those who help us to maximize the benefits of our place in our common biosphere.

That's an answer that goes on and on with other positive benefits. I am not sure if that is an answer to your question or a speech. If it's a speech, I am always glad to give a speech like that! But I would welcome your follow-up question, if you dare to ask one after a long answer like that."

Linda responded with high respect when she said, "I have no doubt but that, you too, have caught the torch that Granddad passed along.

So, another question has to do with that impressive sculpture at the corner of the World Citizen Center - what does it represent?"

"Wow," Dr. Logan said, "you are inviting me to speak about something that I like talking about. What does it represent? In one sense those three triangles and towering pylons are somewhat like abstract art, you can give them your own meaning. But for me, that sculpture represents our quest to align our story with the magnificence of the indescribably amazing universe of existence of which we are a part.

The logo/icon is one that Dr. James Kelly, your granddad, created and included in his writing. In short, for him, and for me, it represents the wonder and marvel of the new sacred. It speaks to us of the wisdom of aligning our story with a knowledge-based faith that respects a reach for our highest humanity in our info-tech age. Things that may seem not interconnected are at some scale, things we need to connect in our minds with dreams of a better future. It's something we can signal with our own story. It's something the World Citizen Center can signal with its story. That's why it is there! We shape its meaning by our best dreams.

For me, that futuristic sculpture of three triangles and its three pylons reaching toward the sky connects yesterday and tomorrow as an echo of one of the greatest story-teller teachers in all history who lead a dream that is still waiting to be finished. Dr. Kelly talked about it as an ongoing process. So, while we are reaching for our new tomorrows, we can expect that the oneness of life forces will come together in new ways as a vital energy in our own story. It's the way life works. It's the way we can work with the way life works.

There are no guarantees. We do not know what the future will be like, but we know that the Teacher dared to dream an ongoing dream. It isn't finished yet and that is where we can have a place in the story.

Do I sound like Dr. James Kelly? You would know. You knew him. You have read his books. That sculpture is an icon to dreams.

When I was so highly privileged to be a part of the creation of the prospectus for the World Citizen Center, I asked the architect to incorporate the three triangles into the plans. It represents the marvel of our molecular existence. It represents the grandeur of a starry sky in which this little planet exists. It reflects the wisdom of living by a faith that respects the way we can align our story with the magnificence of a knowledge-based faith and the new sacred. No wonder one of the words in Dr. Kelly's Big Ten Universal

Qualities is respect. And no wonder I am excited about having the high privileged of being a part of the World Citizen Center. I believe in it. I have great hopes for what it can do to help us build a great future.

What I am eager to hear is what Steve has to say about a new phase and how all of us may be privileged to have a part in it.

So, Steve, maybe you can tell us what you have on the horizon of dreams that can be represented by that majestic icon of new tomorrows."

Steve pushed away from the table and began eagerly. "The ideas we have been working with up to now have been simple enough to be profound. And, now once again, that may be the case. What we dream and plan must have that element of simplicity and basic understanding of who we are and what dreams we dare to put into action. As I have dreamed and re-dreamed this new phase, I have talked to myself and I keep saying, 'For this new plan to work it must be simple and basic. That is my hope as I present the plan for consideration by people whose own ideas and evaluations I respect highly.

But to venture on, the ideas I have in mind boil down to training teachers to teach the Big Ten Universal Qualities in many respective places and styles of teaching. The overall objective is to create a living legacy of Granddad's dream of getting the Big Ten taught in all the learning centers of the world, in the home, in our worship centers, our schools, clubs, business planning retreats, youth programs, etc. wherever these overarching identity markers can be taught and chosen to lead the way to unparalleled great new tomorrows.

I propose that we have a launch banquet for presenting the plan for training teachers to teach the Big Ten.

Along with this teaching part, and in order to reach a wide audience, I propose that we have Big Ten Success Rallies for large audiences, focused on parents, young people, and career leaders.

So, I propose to bring Jenny and Linda on board as a team to design a series of training events to teach teachers to teach the Big Ten Universal Qualities,. And I propose to bring Clark and Brian on board to launch enthusiastic energized Big Ten Success Rallies. These skilled partners can help the World Citizen Center carry Dr. James Kelly's dream forward so that millions will be invited to make the Big Ten Universal Qualities the identity markers they choose for their successful place in humanity's ongoing story.

The teaching part may expand later, but in the beginning, I propose that we begin to teach teachers so they in turn are trained to go out and set up their own little learning events where they teach the Big Ten. This could be a part of Sunday School classes for short term units. It could be of the same nature for school teachers who will make the Big Ten a part of their ongoing classes, like in social studies, or career skills. This short-term learning event could be a part of Boy Scout or Girl Scout programs and summer camps. A teacher could get a group of children together in his or her home. Parents can create home classes where they teach the Big ten qualities to fellow parents.

I propose that we have the Big Ten Success Rallies in some of the Family Life Centers of large churches, where many people will not only learn the principles of success embodied in living by the Big Ten, but will see the need for children to learn the same principles on their level. In turn, they will be eager to have their children be a part of programs where they can learn about and choose the Big Ten as the ABC's for their identity.

In these rallies parents, young career people, and young people will be motivated to reset their identity by the success dynamics energized by the Big Ten Universal Qualities.

For this dream, I hope we can draw on the skills base that Linda and Jenny have in teaching.

I hope we can draw on the promotion skills that Clark and Brian have for launching Big Ten Success Rallies.

All the while, in both programs, we will make all of the *A Place In The Story* books available so people can purchase these books and take them home and read them in their family settings so they will be inspired to try living out the Big Ten qualities in their own success stories.

I caution myself, and need to caution all of us, that we need to start small and local and to keep our planning so simple and basic that it carries a sense of being so important it will grow and expand until it reaches millions.

Now, Dr. Logan, here's one critical part. Are you, and the board of directors of your Vision Foundation, ready to come on board with this dream and fund it at a level that is more than venture capital, but as a way to help many people be world citizens? Can you see yourself and your Vision Foundation as an intentional investor in this way to shape the future?

And the other critical part is if Clark and Jenny, and Brian and Linda, will join in this quest, so that after we draw up more specific plans and agreements, all of us will be ready to ask together, 'When can we get started?'"

A respectful pause followed before Steve spoke again. "Up here on Eagles View Mountain is where our dreams began to be shaped into plans. Down there is where they took place. Out there is where we want to take the dream forward so that no boy or girl in Alpine, or the region beyond, or in the world, will ever have to say that they were not taught the Big Ten Universal Qualities as an overarching framework for identity and success. Out there, in our home, school, church, club, or social network, in big success rallies, the Big Ten Universal Qualities can be learned and embraced as the qualities that lead to a higher humanity. No matter what their culture or career track, these are the qualities which will set their story on a higher level for successful achievement.

Our mission, then is to live on the leading edge of the future. Our goal is to help people choose the Big Ten Universal Qualities as a framework for a knowledge-based faith that links our science and technology with a positive lifting identity, so that together they lead to successful living.

We live in an age of rapid change, especially in science and technology. More and more, it is up to us to choose and shape our own story by those ABC qualities that make us into world citizens. This is our call from the future!

So a question for Clark and Jenny, and for Brian and Linda is, 'Can you see yourself in this dream as a call from your new tomorrows?

And the question for all of us is, "Will we dare to begin?"

CHAPTER FOUR

The Big Ten World Citizen Teachers Banquet

LIKE THE GRAND EVENT THAT LAUNCHED THE OPENING OF THE World Citizen Center earlier, the Big Ten World Citizen Teachers Banquet was an event that indicated big plans. The tables were spread with white tablecloths and dinnerware. The servers were wearing white dinner jackets and black ties, all trained in the art of serving with style, but more importantly with the skill of kindness and caring.

One variation from the earlier World Citizen Center launch banquet was that just as people were finishing their desert, several fifth grade students marched on stage with zestful enthusiasm, turned to the audience, and waited until their director turned to the pianist and gave the cue, then directed them in an enthusiastic presentation of a song that named all ten of the Big Ten Universal Qualities.

There's a kindness for every pathway,
    Honesty in all we say.
There's respect for every caring,
    Qualities that lead the way.
There is vision on new horizons,
    We can climb and look to see,
The new sacred ever nearer,
    Waiting now for you and me.

Collaboration is in our future,
    Tolerance and integrity.
Fairness leads tomorrow,
    Joining with diplomacy.
Nobility crowns our heroes,
    Honoring highest qualities,
The new sacred ever nearer,
    Waiting now for you and me.

We can claim each new promise,
    As one we can make to be,
Turning each old ending,
    Into paths we begin anew.
There is hope in each tomorrow,
    We can claim for our today,
The new sacred ever nearer,
    Waiting now for you and me.

They walked off stage with the same intentional energy they had entered, while the audience heralded them with a lengthening applause.

Steve walked to center stage and paused until he had the full attention of his audience. "You may recognize that song as one that comes from the book, *A Place In The Story*. It was presented by Jenny Henderson's fifth grade class at the school where she teaches. You will be privileged to hear Jenny speak to you later in the evening. But what a wonderful introduction. It announces the theme that is at the center of tonight's launch event for Big Ten World Citizen Teachers.

Living by the Big Ten qualities is a learned skill. It's like playing a violin or playing baseball or reading, those skills have to be learned. Many skills are learned from professionally trained teachers. But parents are also teachers. They are among the first teachers and often the most important.

Parents, your children are your students. In day to day living, they listen to your words and watch the way you live. They are most fortunate if you know how to be successful, not just as wage earners, but successful in living out the Big Ten qualities by being kind, caring, honest, and respectful – when you show how to collaborate with tolerance and fairness – when you demonstrate integrity – when you show how to live with diplomacy and nobility.

If these are the qualities you would like for your children to learn at places beyond the home, like classes at school or church or in their clubs, you will be interested in hearing about the bold plans we are announcing here this evening.

We are beginning a new program here in which teachers will be trained to be Big Ten Teachers. It is an opportunity for persons who may already be teachers in schools, or Sunday schools, or leaders in clubs, or community programs to become teachers of with a special focus - they will be trained to teach the Big Ten Universal Qualities. So, parents, this is good news. Your children will have opportunities to learn from these special teachers the ABC's of successful living.

Teachers who lead these classes are ready to make learning real fun. We can announce here tonight that Jenny Henderson and Linda Kelly have chosen to be leaders in this new program. They are skilled teachers already. If any of you here want to learn to teach these skills, you will have the opportunity to apply tonight to be in their classes and become certified Big Ten World Citizen Teachers. Jenny and Linda are excited about the ways they can make these events delightful fun for all those who participate in these short-term classes. And while the main emphasis will be to train teachers of children, there will be opportunities for adults, especially parents, to be a part of these classes, so they can create some learning events that help them reset their identity aligned with the Big Ten qualities!

These classes will begin immediately. You can sign up tonight. In turn. you can begin to plan for ways you can begin your own Big Ten Success classes, unique to your settings and opportunities. It can be as simple as getting a half dozen children together in your neighborhood, or when a small group of parents who want to form a learning group, get together to form Big Ten learning classes in each others homes.

Then one year from now we will have another banquet where those who teach these classes, and those who have been these classes, and those who have been to a Big Ten Yardstick Success

Rally will share their personal stories about the positive difference these have made in their lives.

Everything has a learning curve. To be sure, we will have our own as we try and learn together. This is our plan, and this is the launch event! It is a plan that can be simple enough and flexible enough to be successful. It's a fulfillment of the dream of Dr. James Kelly that the Big Ten Universal Qualities be taught in all the learning centers of the world so that no child will ever have to say, "I never was taught the Big Ten qualities as part of my identity and my plans for a successful life." Instead, they will define themselves as the Big Ten Generation.

There will be three expectations if you choose to become a Big Ten success teacher. You will be expected to read all of Dr. Kelly's books. You will be expected to make this positive philosophy of life and the Big Ten qualities a real part of your story. And, you will be encouraged to find places and ways you can teach a class on the Big Ten qualities as a certified Big Ten Teacher.

Scary? Not when you read the books, take these fun classes, and dare to follow in the footsteps of one of the greatest teachers of all time, who taught that, "While you are asking, it will be given you; while you are seeking, you will find; and while you are knocking, it will be opened to you."

Who should be excited about this opportunity? Parents!

In addition to training a multitude of teachers, who want to learn to teach the Big Ten, we will have a series of Big Ten Success Rallies, where we bring together large crowds of parents, youth, and career people to listen to outstanding speakers who have tried these qualities in their own story and are ready to tell how those qualities have been a new beginning in their success story. We propose to have these in churches where they have the facilities to hold a rally of this magnitude.

These rallies will be launched by Clark Henderson and Brian Kelly. These leaders already have skills for planning events and will bring in speakers who can tell their success stories about how they chose to make the Big Ten their self-chosen identity markers.

Our plans are big. They are daring. But they have great potential to have a multiplying effect so that, in a wide variety of ways, we can learn how to make the Big Ten Universal Qualities a measuring template for more successful living.

In addition to calling these rallies a Big Ten Success Rally, we think they may also be called the Yardstick Rallies. Why? We will boldly print the words of the Big Ten Universal Qualities on yardsticks and give them to each person who attends these rallies. We already know about the golden rule being printed on rulers. We will now print the Big Ten qualities on yardsticks as the way to measure for wholesome, honorable success!

While the main focus of the Big Ten Teaching program will be on teachers and children, the focus of the Big Ten Success Rallies will be on young people and parents and career leaders. Young people are at a critical time for shaping their chosen identity. They need the inner guidance of the Big Ten qualities to help them build wise and wholesome goals for success. And it's parents who need to make the Big Ten qualities real in the home. Parents are teachers. So one of the important learning centers is the home.

Our bold plans are to make Dr. Kelly's dream of teaching the

Big Ten Universal Qualities in the learning centers of the world, become real.

Will we ever achieve that objective? What's your best guess? What we can do is begin and get as close as we can to achieving this idealistic dream. What we know is that we will never get there unless we begin. We have begun. It's an ongoing dream. It's one you can join!

CHAPTER FIVE

The Yardstick Success Rally

THE IDEA OF CALLING THE BIG TEN SUCCESS RALLIES, THE YARDSTICK Success Rally was a development that was suggested in a fun sort of way, but after that, no one was willing to turn it loose. It fit! It summarized what the rallies were all about - a way of measuring by those qualities which are in fact, a universal yardstick. And the idea that everyone who attended would be given a yardstick, with the words of the Big Ten printed on them, would give the rallies a unique way of making people feel they already know the positive message of the rally would be something to measure by for their own success story.

The first rally was set to be held in the city of Kinston, forty miles north of Alpine. The assumption was that people would travel many miles to be a part of a big success rally, especially one billed as a rally for parents, and for young people who were asked to bring their boyfriend or girlfriend. Dr. David Logan had been to several success rallies, mostly designed for the business and professional community with a dollar mark promise, but he wanted this one to be different. It would simple be open to anyone who wanted to build a better future by choosing ten words to shape their identity for a more successful life.

The Family Life Center at University Church in Kinston was uniquely located and had facilities that could seat a thousand people. Along with that, it was known as the church in the city that people looked to for leading-edge thinking. The people of the church welcomed having an event that was billed as A FOCUS ON A SUCCESSFUL FUTURE, and FREE AND OPEN TO THE PUBLIC.

In success rallies that Dr. Logan had attended, he liked it when the speakers would walk onto an open stage and immediately have the full attention of the audience.

That was the way the first Big Ten Success Rally opened in Kinston. Steve Kelly walked briskly to center stage, holding up his yardstick up like a cheerleader with a baton, leading athletes at the opening of the Olympics! All the seats were filled. The muffled sound of the audience grew quiet quickly when they saw Steve come on stage. With his yardstick held high, Steve said, "Each of you was given a yardstick! So, are ready to measure.? If so, hold it up and say, 'LET'S MEASURE!'

Following that immediate enthusiastic response, Steve said, "I think I heard you, but would you stand and say it again? Immediately that audience stood and said, 'LET'S MEASURE!' Steve said, "I heard you that time, but maybe they didn't hear you all way across the city. Could you say it again? 'LET'S MEASURE!' The roar that sounded was like that of the crowd at a ballgame when a player had just hit the ball into the bleachers for a homerun!

After Steve motioned for them to be seated, he said, "We have indeed come here to measure! We have come to measure for success - your success as a young person, your success as a parent, your success in your career, whatever that place may be in your journey story. And we have some outstanding people who will help us measure. In a moment we will bring them on stage to help us reset our best dreams and explore how we can give great dreams their best chance to happen!

We live in the greatest age the human family has ever known! That age will reach its full potential as we embrace a knowledge-based faith informed by science, technology, and the Big Ten Universal Qualities, the qualities which are boldly printed on your yardstick. Those qualities belong to the world family! They are the qualities we can measure by so we are one of millions who are choosing to help make this the greatest age in all the human story. How about if we read the words printed on your yardsticks together! KINDNESS, CARING, HONESTY, INTEGRITY, COLLABORATION, TOLERANCE, FAIRNESS, INTEGRITY, DIPLOMACY, NOBILITY!

Steve had the full attention of the packed audience as he continued.

"This is the first of many Yardstick Success Rallies. This is a way to launch ten qualities onto a world stage to help us be world citizens. Where? Wherever each of us lives our story. It is location-neutral, but identity-specific. It gives each of us our own unique chance to see how ten words can shape our identity so they help us to be successful in our digital-information-molecular age. These are universal qualities which give churches and other organizations a way to highlight those qualities which make their people more successful as a compliment to whatever their faith orientation may be!

Dr. James Kelly, my granddad, had a dream that the Big Ten Universal Qualities could be taught in all the learning centers of the world. This rally is one of those centers! You are here at a strategic time! We are taking one giant step forward for mankind!

The speakers you will hear are no ordinary speakers. They are persons who have excelled in their respective professions. You will hear them saying many of the things you would hear at most any success rally. Beyond that, they speak out of a context of having read all of the *A Place In The Story* books and have made a personal effort to incorporate a quality-based-living approach into their own daily life. Because of that, they will present a broad understanding of who we are, but focused anew in the Big Ten qualities.

There is something that is special about these speakers. They want no fee for speaking. They are aware of the mission of the World Citizen Center and want to be a part of its growing influence for good. In some rallies success speakers get thousands of dollars for one appearance. Our speakers believe in what we are doing so much that they choose not to receive any fee at all, and are here at their own expense. This not only helps us to expand these rallies to other regions as free and open to the public, but give these leaders a platform for sharing their insights about how to make a better world.

Before I present our fist speaker, I want to define the paradigm out of which we see our place in the story as leaders of the World Citizen Center. In his books, Dr. Kelly respects the progression of science and technology and the tremendous difference these have made in the way we see who we are and become, in our digital-information-molecular age. In fact, I can do no better introduction to this than to quote from his book, *New Tomorrows*. Dr. Kelly says, 'Now that we are experiencing the obsolescence of traditional authority-based religion, we need to build something of even greater promise. I believe it is time to build an identity based in a knowledge-based faith, informed by science and technology, and the Big Ten Universal Qualities. If this framework of identity defines the persons we seek to become, we will build a noble future that we can be proud to claim as our new tomorrows story.'

We started the World Citizen Center with a very local audience in Alpine. The speakers at that opening banquet are so in step with the mission of the center that they have offered to tell their story on a larger stage. With some repetition of what they said then, they have continued to make the Big Ten Universal Qualities a part of their lives, and are eager to share more of their story now.

These ten qualities may be simple enough that, when they are chosen by the people of the world as a framework for identity that overarches our religions, politics, and cultures, they will help millions to be more successful. When we live out the Big Ten Universal Qualities, that may be the finest gift we can make to the human family in its progression to a higher humanity. We can help heal the hurts and scars of the past by being one the future's Big Ten world citizens. Automatic and Easy? No. But so needed in our time? Yes. Very much so in our age of progressive change! We all can be a part of this yardstick world citizen generation!

Here now is one of the speakers who can help us. His story is a living example of the influence of the Big Ten qualities. I now present to you a key leader in this rally, Mr. Clark Henderson. Clark, bring your yardstick and come to tell us your story!"

Clark Henderson walked on stage quickly, holding his yardstick in the middle and twisting it back and forth like a baton. "I have one too," he said as he turned to the applauding audience. He launched into his presentation saying, "Success. What is success? Many people have tried to define it. I have my own definition. It's being confident about who you are as measured by the ten words of the Big Ten Universal Qualities printed on your yardstick.

Now these words are not brand new to me. I grew up with them. I was measuring by them before I knew about them as the ten words on a yardstick. My parents were Big Ten people before they knew how to list them in ten words. I was measuring by them in my early career when I was privileged to find the greatest girl on campus and was privileged to marry her. That was success already for me.

Then together, right out of our MBA degrees, we began to measure by our good jobs with good pay that allowed us to do up-scale living and drive prestige cars. We measured by, and liked to be around, people who had the same relish for that kind of success.

Then I got a new view of success. My parents died. I reflected deeply on their story. They didn't have a yardstick with those words on it, but they lived by those words. When Jenny and I went back out to the apple farm after both of them had died, we began to see what they had measured by. It was about being honest and fair. It was about kindness and caring. It was about service and being a friend to everyone.

For Dad, it meant being a good apple farmer who tried to be a true friend to all those who worked for him and to all those who came to the apple shed to buy apples and cider. He loved to sit on the porch of the apple shed and talk to his customers. He would walk with them out to their vehicles, as though each of them was a very special friend.

As for Mother, she was a teacher of fifth grade children in public school. She loved the children and they loved her. She was more than just their teacher; she was their friend, and they knew it.

Suddenly the big salaries Jenny and I liked to brag about and the advancements in our careers began to look different, to much like gloss and shine, and not enough about being the kind of people my parents were. When I asked Jenny what she thought we ought to do with the apple farm, she said,, "Move out here and keep it going."

"Are you serious? I asked immediately in surprise.

"Yes, I am," she said. "Your parents were the most honorable people I have ever known. If we could live so that someone could say the same about us when our story is completed, I think that would mean we had been successful. We would have used our skills and knowledge to link us with genuine honor."

I was surprised at her immediate answer, that we should move back out here to the apple farm. But what did we do? We moved to the farm. She became a fifth grade teacher like my mother had been. I became an apple farmer like my Dad. We haven't gotten rich yet. Never will. But we are rich in the best sense of our humanity as two people who are trying to add to the common good in the human family.

After we moved back we became a part of the World Citizen Church. We learned about Dr. James Kelly and his books, and read all of them. Then Jenny got that rare privilege of helping Dr. Kelly with his dream that the Big Ten qualities be taught in all the learning centers of the world. And I got the opportunity to help create these Yardstick Success Rallies. Neither of us hesitated for a moment. We said, 'yes.' We knew we wanted to be a part of this new venture and the promise of a better tomorrow..

What a privilege to be standing here today telling you our story. What a privilege to talk to young people and parents about the kind of success that is defined by the Big Ten qualities. What a privilege to hold up a Big Ten yardstick and measure by it!

Not everybody has an apple farm, but everyone has some kind of parallel to it where they can share their gifts and skills in a service of dignity and respect. That's success!

So, here's the success principle. Instead of measuring from the past, measure from the future. We are indebted to the past, but we owe more to the future. To build that future, discover your talents and abilities. Develop them to a high level. Then find your ways to make them real through honorable service somewhere that is right for you. Don't try to keep life, give it away. It may, or may not, make you wealthy, but you will be rich - yardstick rich!"

Clark waved his yardstick as he began to march off stage, to the applause of an admiring audience.

While Clark was walking off the stage, the next speaker was beginning to walk on. That's when Clark abruptly stopped and faced the new speaker. He said, "Brian, you can't go out there yet. You don't have your yardstick."

The audience grew silent suddenly as they watched the little drama. "But I have to go on. I'm the next speaker. I have a yardstick, just not with me now."

"Here. Take mine," Clark said. "These yardsticks are interchangeable. They measure the same for everyone. I'll get another one."

The audience burst into applause as Brian took the yardstick and began waving it like a flag pole.

Brian turned to his audience and said, "Wow. That was almost like a little clip from the 'I Love Lucy' show.' You know Lucy and Ricardo. They were always in some kind of ridiculous pickle, but not one they couldn't work out of with the help of two scheming allies like Fred and Helen. With their help, Lucy always had some kind of ridiculous new idea that saved the day."

Brian waved his yardstick again and said, "Thanks Clark. You saved my day. Now I have a yardstick. And I have a yardstick story. Clark talked about having read the stories that Dr. James Kelly tells in his books. But I haven't just read them, I heard Dr. Kelly tell his stories on the porch at his farmhouse. All of my cousins sat there and listened to Granddad tell stories that were unforgettable metaphors for turning old endings into new beginnings. Granddad's stories gave us something to measure by, especially one. It was a story in which God asked Moses to measure, not by the past, but by the future, to measure by new possibilities, to go back up the mountain!

Let me tell you that story like Granddad told it. I'll need to adapt it and abbreviate it a little. There was Moses with his new little nation out there in the desert and needing to go forward to new possibilities. And God was saying, 'Cut two tables of stone and go up into the peaks of Mount Sinai and I will give you ten commandments to lead you and your little nation forward to a new tomorrow.

So Moses recruited a strong young man to help him carry those stones as they trekked up to the top of the mountain. Up there, in their dream-ahead mountains, their future dreams were put into ten commandments and etched onto those two stone tablets. Then they went back down the mountain, excited and filled with visions of great new tomorrows. But back to camp, what did they see? They saw their people dancing around a god of yesterday, a god of Egypt. They had asked Moses' brother, Aaron, to make them a god from the past. So that leader from the past made them a gold bull and set it up as their god to follow.

When Moses saw that god from yesterday standing there and being celebrated, he could hardly believe what he was seeing. Here he was with ten guidelines to a great future and those people were dancing around a god of the past.

'What is your reference?' Moses wanted to know. 'Are you to be defined by who you have been or by who you can become? We, who refused to bow to Pharaoh, will we now bow to his gods? If that is all we dared and dreamed for, we may as well have stayed in Egypt!'

Moses held up the stones on which it was written, 'you shall not make yourself a graven image.' But they had done just that. They were dancing around an idol of yesterday! In his hands Moses was holding up a dream for tomorrow. In a moment of disappointment, Moses thrust the stone to the ground. And to his utter surprise, his precious commandments broke into pieces. Embarrassed and regretful, Moses stepped across those broken commandments and retreated to his tent.

That's when Aaron and some other leaders came to his tent and said, 'Now, Moses, don't take it so hard. If can't remember what was on those stones we can just recall some of the laws of Egypt and go by them. It's no big deal.'

'But it is a big deal!', Moses thundered back. 'We who would not be slaves of Pharaoh, will we now be slaves of his gods? What is to be our reference? To the past or to the future? Will we be defined by who we have been, or by who we can be? We can never be our best and face our new challenges when we are only measuring by the past. We must measure by our best future - by our dreams of new tomorrows!'

The next morning as the sun was coming up, Moses stepped out of his tent and quietly heard God speaking to him, saying, 'Moses. Moses, cut out two stone tablets like the first ones and meet me at the top of the mountain.'

That's when Moses said, 'God, you have to be kidding. I can't do that. I have humiliated myself before those people. And I am scared - cold sweat scared. I have been discredited. I am no leader now. I am a failure. You don't expect me to try again, do you?'

And God said, 'Yeeeess!'

So, Moses cut out two new stones and went back up the mountain to dream again. When he came back down the mountain, he was a new Moses. He was a man who had refused to stop at embarrassment and failure. He had a new mission and a new identity. Instead of saying, 'I can't,' he was saying, 'I can.'"

Brian stopped, paused a moment, looked across his audience and asked, 'Are you Moses? Are you facing discouragement in the face of the changes of our time? Are you afraid of failure? Cold-sweat scared, when you wake up at night? Are you discouraged about your career? Have you been disappointed in your own story? Which Moses are you? The one saying, 'I can't.' or the one saying, 'I can,' ready to go back up your mountain again?

Life has lots of mountains to climb back up. It's easy to look at the broken stones at our feet and say, 'I can't.' But the Moses of new tomorrows is the ones who says, 'I can.' and then dares to go back up the mountain.

So you had a breakup with your boyfriend or girlfriend, and you are hurt, and disappointed. That is no quitting place. Rebuild relationships. Build new relationships. Give the future its best chance. Say it to yourself, 'I can.' Then say it again, 'I can! I can!'

So what? There are broken stones in your story, but are you going to measure by the past, or by the future? What is your reference? To what has been, or to what can be?

We live at a time when it is immensely important to face our mountains with an 'I can' mindset and dare to dream our best dreams for new tomorrows. The developments in science and technology give each of us new tools to work with. And now we have ten new word tools to use, the Big Ten Universal Qualities,that anyone, anywhere, at anytime can choose to guide us to the best we can be. These ten words can be an umbrella of qualities to measure by. They keep us reaching for those successes that come when we go back up our mountains!

I knew Vernon, back when his wife had died, and he was heartbroken and discouraged. But he began to ask himself, 'Am I to measure by what has been? Or am I to measure by the best story I can create that extends our story?' Out of his disappointment and loss, Vernon realized his couldn't take hold of the future unless he turned loose of the past. It was his mountain to climb.

I knew Betsy. She felt humiliated. She failed the ninth grade. But her teacher sat down beside her and said, 'Betsy, what are you good at? What are your signature strengths? What skill would you most like to develop as your achievement markers? Tell yourself what that is and then tell yourself, 'I can! I can develop that skill. I can make a new beginning. I can go back up the mountain!'

Do you have a mountain to climb? What are you saying to your mountain? Find your way to say, 'I can!' and head back up the mountain.

I have been working in a college admissions office. Some of those who began college will graduate. Some will fail or just drop out. But in either category they dare not drop out on a successful life. There are still mountains to climb - ten qualities that are their own degrees in excellence. Wherever the journey leads you will need to try and try again. Adapt. Adjust. Just don't quit. Let your story be defined by who you can be when you choose to etch ten words into your identity framework and make them your call to go back up the mountain. Hold your identity yardstick high and let those ten words be your reference to new tomorrows as part of the Big Ten World Citizen Generation!

You know President Jimmy Carter's story - a one-time president who was never to be celebrated as one of the great two-term presidents. But you also know his story that, beyond that disappointment, he became one of the world's most helpful and positive leaders, and wrote more than twenty books to tell his story and declare his dreams.

You know President Clinton's big failed moment. But who does not recognize the far reaching influence of the Clinton Initiative in which thousands of people have joined with him to make a difference for good in the world.

There are many people who have to learn to handle tough situations as a positive rebound. There are mountains to climb back up.

What's your mountain? There are ten guiding markers that can help you climb! Keep your Big Ten Yardstick handy.

Now I get to introduce you to a mountain climber. She climbs mountains in her laboratory. But right now, she's here and ready to tell her story, and stories about other almost silent mountain climbers. Welcome, Dr. Kara Marcel!"

When Kara Marcel walked on to the stage she held up her yardstick and said, "Yes. I have my yardstick."

When Kara got to the center of the stage she paused in a very relaxed manner, as though she was very much at home in speaking to a large audience. "Yes, I have my yardstick and I cherish it. I value the ten words listed on it.

I am a family life counselor. Those ten words are at the center of what my work is all about. I work at the broken edges of dreams and relationships. But I also work at the leading edge of new tomorrows. When I work with my people I can't restore the brokenness of yesterday, but I can help people reset tomorrow. Even if we never get up to the utopian level of our dreams, all of us can keep reaching to the person we would like to be.

Along with all the speakers who were asked to be a part of the Big Ten Success Rallies, I was asked to read Dr. James Kelly's books. I have read some sections more than once. I wish I had been privileged to have had them when I was in college. I wish I had them when I began my counseling service. But wishing doesn't make it that way. Yesterday is always past, but there is always today. I am glad that I have these words now. They are so on target with what my life and what my counseling service is all about. They are healthcare books. So, I not only read them again, but I prescribe them for my clients. They supplement and multiply my efforts, big time. Families may get even more help from reading those books than they do from talking with me.

Let me explain. At birth, not all, but most people's story goes uphill for a good while, some more than others. Then there is that plateau or drop off. Sooner or later, life goes downhill and problems become part of the story. We can't retain our youth. We can't restore it. But we can learn to build new beginnings beyond old endings. Yesterday, whatever it was like, is past. But finding new tomorrows is a kind of birth.

I help families deal with problems and issues. I help them reset healthy positive expectations. Here is something I am discovering again and again. The more my people adopt the Big Ten qualities, the more likely they are to find healing in their family relationships. That puts me in the healing business. We learn from the past, but we can define the future with new words tools.

A surgeon has new tools, thanks to technology. A mechanic has new tools, even digital tools, that diagnose a car's problems. A teacher gets new books and computers.

What kind of new tools do family life counselors get? We get the Big Ten Universal Qualities! And after this conference, guess what my clients will get on their first visit in my office. They will get a Big Ten yardstick and be asked to read the *A Place In The Story* books.

I know that one of the upcoming speaker is a neurologist, but I need to say, in line with what he will talk about, is that the brain is plastic, that it can be reset. That thesis is basic in my line of work. No one can live a good life without having to reset his or her identity inputs to the brain from time to time. I, along with psychologists and psychiatrist, deal with people's depression. Depression is an expression of a fear scenario, and fear is often a fallout from depression. Negative thoughts and self-images keep recycling. But the more we can make positive thinking the attitudes and emotional markers we input to the brain, the less depression and fear we will be dealing with. With less fear and a more positive outlook on life, we will be healthier and add to good emotional health in our families.

So, parents, that's why it is so important for you to give praise and repeated encouragement to your children. No, don't praise them when they don't deserve it, but when there is anything to praise, then praise it, and never stop no matter how old they are.

Kindness is not only the first word of the Big Ten, but it is basic, and linked to all the other words. And kindness and caring begin at home. It is highly important for parents to be kind and cordial, respectful, fair, tolerant, and honest with their children. Caring enough about your children to be kind to them is mostly a silent force but highly important in their healthy identity. And it's so simple. Anybody can be kind!.

Now, young people, turn what I just said to parents around. If you are fortunate enough to have reasonable good parents, respect them for that by being kind to them. Yes, they are from another generation and they just can't catch up with lots of change, but you can be respectful and kind to them. Kindness and caring, honesty and respect are basic in a healthy family. Be sure you are doing your part. Give kindness away as what you can add.

Then there's that big word, collaboration for both parents and young people. Work together. Networking and helping each other achieve goals is big business on small stages, especially on the home and family stage. And it makes family life so much more rewarding, and more fun.

Now, if you think I am overplaying the importance of the Big Ten, rethink that. These ten qualities are at the heart of a healthy identity. They are at the heart of self-development. There's a reason I prescribe them. They work.

I have one more emphasis to make. Make learning a part of the ongoing agenda in your family. Nurture it. Explore newness. Learn to have a faith that is bigger than your differences, a faith that overarches whatever your religion, politics, or culture may be.

I am almost at that point in my profession where I will not take on a new family or individual unless they are willing to read Dr. Kelly's books. Talk about marriage problems, many of them will cease to exist when these qualities are moved front and center in relationships. These ten qualities help us to give our best, and when we give our best, it tends to come back to us.

In conclusion, what I have said here is not new to success rallies. But I am so glad to have a chance to be a part of a rally that is a Big Ten Universal Qualities Rally - a Yardstick Success Rally!"

When Kara said that, the audience didn't wait – they broke into an affirming applause as she walked off stage, waving her yardstick.

Steve came immediately to the stage and said, "This is great and there's more to come. But, now it's break time. Don't go anywhere. Don't you dare leave this rally. There is more to come that is a part of your success story."

CHAPTER SIX

New Paradigms

AMID THE NOISY MUFFLE OF A THOUSAND PEOPLE'S CONVERSATION
with each other, Steve lifted his yardstick and waited for people to
realize it was a request for silence.

"I know," he began, "it's a bit of a stretch to ask a minister to
be a part of this rally. Year after year, and Sunday after Sunday,
they speak out of a context in which a book from yesterday is used
to address people of today. But what I know is that some ministers
make that transition and align stories from the past as metaphors for
the future. They move from an authority approach to religion, over
to a high respect for the progression of knowledge which is forever
changing our identity reference to immanence. They speak out of
a context, where the quest is to have a faith which so overarches
religion that it becomes a call from the new sacred. Ministers like
this are asking their people to build a faith that honors the past by
building a new and better future. It's a new paradigm for thinking.

Our next speaker is that kind of leader and thinker. With great respect for his leadership, I invite our next speaker to the platform. And, yes, he had better bring his yardstick, or he will be in water too deep to measure. I kid, of course. Join me in welcoming Rev. Stuart Finelli to the platform.

Rev. Finelli came to the platform holding out his yardstick as though he were measuring an invisible something on his wrist.

'What am I measuring?' he asked. "There is no way to do it fully, but I am measuring what we have become acutely aware of, the progression of time and new ways of thinking. The human family has progressed from an age when even the best thinkers in the human family knew so little about the nature of existence, and who they were, just barely beyond survival and existing. When we compare that with the advance in knowledge and the tools of technology in just the last ten years, we are ready to say, how did we ever get here?' It makes us acutely aware of the progression of science and technology. Does our faith need to reflect these changes? Indeed it does. For some, there is resistance, bolstered by the claim that the sacred comes from the past. Others are more open and say that in order to be honest, our faith must not just keep up with the times, but keep leading the times. These leading thinkers are more connected to what we can do that is better than what we have already done. They are trying to define who we are in terms of the thesis Dr. Kelly set forth in which we are called to have a knowledge-based faith, informed by science, technology, and the Big Ten Universal Qualities.

So, I am ever so glad to have a rally where the focus is on the kind of success, which not only recognizes the tremendous significance of science and technology, but defines a successful life in terms of qualities-based living. Our faith not only needs to keep up with our science, it must lead the way in defining how science and technology can support our reach for our highest humanity. It's a faith where we learn from the past, but also learn from the future, where we learn from what we have been, but even more significantly, from who we can become.

In that progression I recognize, and highly value, the great Teacher of a faith who envisioned a future beyond his time, Jesus of Nazareth. So I must not fence him in by paradigms which were so often frozen in yesterday's orthodoxy. Instead, I try to learn from that Teacher and his kingdom of heaven dream that there must be ongoing development of our identity. That is the vision we are called to advance in our digital-technological-information age.

Our faith will lead us forward better when we ask of our science and technology and all the new tools given to us, that they not only make us more technologically advanced, but make us more human! In that new sacred, the template we measure by needs to be more humanitarian and less theological, with more imminence and less than transcendence so we see how to serve the age of newness, age after emerging age.

This is indeed the greatest age the human family has ever known to link our technology and our qualities. It's a faith in which, as Dr. Kelly says in his books again and again, 'what we plan to give to life becomes our request of life.'

I am the first of four speakers who represent the crossover of many disciplines of study and experience that are blending into philosophy. So three of us will remain on stage while each successive speaker brings in related viewpoints. Let me move aside so that a speaker who represents the tremendous work being done in brain science can expand our understanding of who we are. Would you welcome a neurologist to the stage, yardstick or no yardstick, please welcome Dr. Marston Novak from the New Frontiers School of Medicine.

Dr. Novak came on stage carrying a small microscope.

He said, "I didn't bring a yardstick, but I did bring a measuring instrument which is having a significant impact of knowing who we are as human beings. It is a small microscope, representing newer and the more powerful ones we use in our time. I brought it to represent the big Magnetic Resonance Imaging tools we now have in our hospitals, and the Electron Scanning Microscopes we use in our research centers which can measure what is happening on an atomic level and what is going on in our brain. Brain science is an important dimension of our understanding of who we are. As never before we know the brain guides our identity, and in turn, our behavior.

With the help of digital scanners, we are learning about the neurons, synapses, and millions of interconnections going on inside our heads. I like what was said of psychiatrist, Norman Doidge, in the introductory pages of his book, *The Brain That Changes Itself,* that a recognition that the brain is plastic is a huge leap in the history of mankind, greater than landing on the moon.

Now we are beginning to map the entire brain. But even when that is completed and we understand that the brain shapes the decisions we make, we are no less accountable for the identity template by which it makes those choices. In fact, it makes us even more responsible for what we think and what we ask our brains to do for us.

I have asked an architect friend to come to help me and the previous speaker connect our stories. Please welcome, Lanier Marcus.

Dr. Novak backed off a couple of steps and stood beside Rev. Finelli. As Mr. Lanier came to center stage he began immediately with a story.

Once upon a time there was a carpenter who built houses in the little town of Nazareth, where he lived. He was also a teacher, but he never forgot about how to build good a house, where the metaphorical question was, 'Where should a good builder begin? With a foundation of sand? No. With rock? Yes.' Then when the rains come and the winds blow, the house will still stand. Remember him? His name is well known. He was a teacher who was always looking ahead. His disciples often called him Master. He talked about building, not just houses, but a kingdom of great dreams where caring and kindness were foundation idea for building a great life.

I am an architect. I design houses. But I listened with interest as our Family Life Counselor, Kara Marcel, talked about brokenness, not just of houses, but the brokenness of families living in houses. I listened to her talk about ten qualities, printed on our yardsticks, that can help heal brokenness in our identity houses.

We have a lot of brokenness in our time in which one segment of the human family tries to impose its religion, or politics, or culture on another segment of the family. But it doesn't work. Never has.

It has led to division and war all across the years. Instead of collaboration and cooperation, for much too long the human story has been a story of division and conflict. We are dismayed that we haven't gotten beyond the paradigm of, respond in kind. Retaliate. Pay back bad for bad. Well, it never has worked and still doesn't.

The Master Teacher knew that didn't work, that instead of being enemies we could be friends. The need is greater than ever before to have a framework for identity that unites and heals our brokenness, an identity which is bigger than our differences in religion, politics, and culture. We need the Big Ten qualities as a template for how we build our lives. We need that collective template for an identity of oneness in the planet Earth family, where respect and tolerance heal our divisions and brokenness, where we are our brothers keeper, where we return good for evil. 'Forgive how many times?' the Teacher asked. Only seven? No. Seventy times seven, always putting the possibilities of healing above and beyond our brokenness. Love your enemy. Care about others. Learn the art of collaboration and kindness, tolerance, and fairness. Build on solid foundations.

We live in the greatest of all ages. We have new tools, new hammers and hoes for better homes and gardens. We can replace evil with good. Put in something better. Show a better picture. Increase the rewards for the good. Build the promise of the future.

I design houses. The blueprint I draw up is the template builders use. Today's human family builder needs a blueprint, a yardstick, with ten qualities for building a great identity in the digital age.

So, let's take our yardsticks home and put them in a conspicious place to remind us of the ten words we need to build a great life as today's World Citizen Generation.

Yes, I read Architectural Digest, that slick magazine where they show beautiful pictures of the latest designs in home furnishings.

It's tomorrows styles today. That's where I like to design houses and write stories, where sunrise dreams define our highest humanity as the dream we keep trying to make become real.

I was asked to present our next speaker. I am pleased to do so. I know him well and respect him highly. Along with two previous speakers, I will remain on stage to suggest the crossover aspect of the interdisciplinary metaphors we need in our digital age.

Our next speaker is a professor at Sagan University. Please welcome, Dr. Dresden Marshall.

Dr. Marshall walked on and began to speak immediately.

"I have done a lot of speaking, but none more special than the request to be a part of this rally in which each of us as speakers were asked to read or reread all the books of the sequels, *A Place In The Story*. It's beginning to come together now. As we bridge our ideas together this is a kind of symposium."

After a brief pause, he said, "Listen. What's that? I hear music and singing. I recognize it. It's the haunting tune and memorable words of the song written by Pete Seeger and Lee Hayes, as sung by Peter, Paul and Mary, *If I Had a Hammer*. If you are old enough to go back a few years, you remember what they were asking for in that song. If they had a hammer, or a bell, or a song to sing, they would be asking for, love between 'my brothers and my sisters, all over this land.' It was a synthesizing cry for a better tomorrow.

We have a new version of that quest. It's the defining reach for a new tomorrow, resounding in ten words, Kindness, Caring, Honesty, Respect, Collaboration, Tolerance, Fairness, Integrity,

Diplomacy, and Nobility. Those words are at the heart of a thesis that asks us to build a better humanity in our time on stage as the new sacred.

In recent times we have created two significant tools which help us understand our place in all molecular and cosmic existence, the Large Hadron Collidor, which searches for the smallest units of our molecular existence, and the Hubble Telescope, which searches the star filled cosmos for the most distant galaxies, in what may be endless existence.

These leave us asking, 'what is unique about our place in these contrasting searches for our existence?' In that quest we put together crossover paradigms which try to show our place in our time in history. When Dr. James Kelly put that identity quest into a sweeping paradigm, he said that we are crossing a great divide from the obsolescence of an authority-based religion, over to a new and growing knowledge-based faith which respects the progression of science and technology and the Big Ten Universal Qualities. It's an open-ended understanding of our place in a story where there is great need for a focus on making our humanity better.

We are at that time in the progression of the human story and the advance of knowledge in which there is a blending of philosophy, science, technology, engineering, social studies and the humanities, aligned through massive information which is now at our fingertips. We need a new Peter, Paul and Mary to sing about our best dreams, aligned in a knowledge-based faith and its ten words, as the new sacred.

If we connect Peter, Paul, and Mary's call for a hammer of love, for our brothers and sisters, we get to Dr. Kelly's dream of having an overarching faith which is so universal that the Big Ten can be taught as the ABC's of identity in all the learning centers of the world.

These ten words are not religious, or political, or cultural. They are identity words that can lead all who choose them to a more successful life. They are yardstick words we can measure by in our reach for our best dreams. For me, they are at the heart of the new sacred.

Our next speaker has been a part of the creation of the World Citizen Center from the time it began as a searching idea.

I am privileged to introduce Dr. Sandra Milan. She is so kind and personable that we just call her, Dr. Sandra. So, welcome the minister of the World Citizen Church, where I attend and listen to her with great respect. Give your greeting applause to Dr. Sandra."

It was a standing welcome as Dr. Sandra walked toward center stage, stopping to shake hands with all four of the previous speakers as they now left the stage.

Dr. Sandra began by saying, "I not only have the privilege, and awesome role of being Dresden Marshall's minister, but of being the minister of David Logan, whose story I am about to tell, all too briefly.

There is a story behind the World Citizen Center and this Yardstick Success Rally. It began when two professors at MIT met outside a restaurant and then went to church together. They were so disappointed by the paradigms in the whole service, its hymns, prayers, and sermon, that one of them was about ready to be a new Martin Luther, and nail a new thesis on the church door. That was

Dr. James Logan. After that disappointing experience, he called and asked me if he could come to see me.

When we met at the church, he said, 'It's so unfair when ministers don't keep up! It's so disrespectful of people when their sermons reflect no change in paradigms from what they would have by reading a fifty year old set of encyclopedias.' Then he launched immediately into the reason for his visit. It was an idea he had gotten while reading Dr. James Kelly's book in which he spoke at a church where they made their fellowship hall into a major conference center and invited a series of guest speakers who could help people upgrade their faith to align with the progression of knowledge. Dr. Layman's question was, 'Why can't we have a conference center like that here at our World Citizen Church?'

That led to a wonderful dream and the creation what is now the magnificent and important World Citizen Center with its leading-edge speakers program. The success of the speakers program has now developed into a new training program in which teachers will learn to teach the Big Ten Universal Qualities. Along with that, a parallel phase has been launched as this, the first of a series of Yardstick Success Rallies.

The thesis is the same one set forth in the books by Dr. Kelly that our faith needs to be a knowledge-based faith, informed by and aligned with the Big Ten Universal Qualities as guidelines for helping us to be successful world citizens right where we live day by day.

A chance to live out those qualities in our personal story in our short lifetime is all we get. That privilege carries a responsibility to develop our skills into a base for service in which we give our best to life as our request of life. In turn, that will become our story that we tell to our children and grandchildren when they say, 'Tell me a story.'

The challenging opportunity for the millions of people in our world family is to discover how to live that story in our time, defined by those qualities which make us worthy of our privileged place in our unparalleled digital-information-molecular age. And for that to happen we need teachers by the millions around the world.

To tell you about this, I want to ask one of the grandchildren of Dr. James Kelly to come and talk about an important expansion of his granddad's dream.

He is our last speaker, so lift your yardsticks high to welcome Dr. Steve Kelly."

When Steve got to the middle of the platform he stood quietly until the applause faded to a respectful silence. He began unhurriedly as he said, "I want to talk to you from the heart, kind of like how my granddad talked to his grandchildren when we gathered on the farmhouse porch.

I am an environmental scientist. I want to talk about the most important environment of our time, the human mind. That is the environment over which we have some personal control, but great responsibility. We live at a time when the identity we choose to guide our mind and its guidance of our future. If we want our best future, we must first envision and define that future as wisely as possible.

I want to say to those of you who are parents, that you have an opportunity to lead the thinking at one of the strategic learning centers of the world, your home.

I want to say to those of you here who are young. You can proudly help make your home one of those learning places. You can be one of those persons who chooses to make this the greatest age in all the human story. You can learn and then model Big Ten qualities as an example of successful living! Perfect? No, but don't ever let that keep you from reaching for the highest level you can. As is often said, 'don't let the perfect stand in the way of the good.' Whatever your family structure and home setting may be, you can build a new partnership for blending science, technology, and a knowledge-based faith into a new sacred in your story.

So, will you as a family do something for me? But far more important, will you do something for yourselves? In your home setting, will you read the engaging and thoughtful fiction books of *A Place In The Story*? Will you devise ways to read them along with each other? And, as you read these story-book visions, will you create some kind of setting for sharing ideas and insights together, maybe at the kitchen table, as your meeting place for dialogue about the ideas you read about in these books? If will do that as a result of being here, this could be the most important rally you will ever attend.

Now let me talk to those of you who are ministers. You were given a special invitation to come to this Big Ten Success Rally. Along with reading your Bible, I am seriously asking you do some reading that keeps you in sync with the most spectacular development in all human history, current science. When you read you create a climate for the brain that connects with the progression of knowledge. So, read MIT's *Technology Review*. Read, *Popular Science, Scientific American Mind, Psychology Today, Science Illustrated* - read a wide spectrum of magazines and books to keep you up-to-date in our rapidly developing world. As a leader of the environment of the mind, your people can rightfully expect you to have a framework of faith that aligns with science, technology, engineering, and math, STEM, and overarches religion, politics, and culture in our digital-information-molecular age. Unless your reading keeps abreast of the times, your pulpit will be echo a knowledge base too much like an obsolete set of old encyclopedias.

The science-fiction movies and books of our time define an imaginary world that is set in the future. But, those who create those science-fiction worlds of tomorrow often employ the best scientists of our time to help them make sure they are staying true to the best and latest in science in the real world. As a real time minister in the digital age, you dare not require of yourself anything less than what science-fiction writers require of themselves.

When I came to Alpine I was privileged to live in a retreat cottage up on the peak of Eagles View Mountain. From there I could look down and see the steeple of a church. When Sunday morning came I made my way back down those winding roads into Alpine and to World Citizen Church. What I discovered was a church which was not only current with growing knowledge, but leading the way to the best of thinking. The minister of that church spoke as a leader of dreams. As she spoke it was obvious she kept up with the progression of knowledge. In addition, she had read all of Dr. James Kelly's books and I could almost hear him speaking anew as she talked about the Big Ten Universal Qualities in terms of making those qualities a part of our own story.

Those of you who are ministers here today can help your church be a church like that which helps parents and young people think in real time and choose the ten universal qualities to measure by.

I have a yardstick. You have a yardstick. We all have a yardstick!

Peter, Paul and Mary sang, about having a hammer and what they could do with it to create a new tomorrow. We have a hammer. We have a Big Ten Yardstick to measure by and shape tomorrow into our success story! It's time to energize our story with sunrise dreams!

As we stand together, show me your yardstick, held high! Now, let's go home and show the world our yardstick!"

Steve stood in the center of the platform and watched the people begin to leave. Sandra walked back on stage and stood beside him and watched. After a prolonged moment of silence, Steve said quietly, "It's not an ending."

"I know," Sandra said, "It's a new beginning."

CHAPTER SEVEN

World Citizen Teachers!

"My name is Steve Kelly. I am privileged to be the Director of the World Citizen Center. On behalf of the center I want to say, 'WELCOME! WELCOME TO A VERY SPECIAL BANQUET. This may be the most unusual banquet you will ever attend. You will have the privilege of getting to know two wonderful teachers, Jenny Henderson, and Linda Kelly.

When you came into the banquet hall you were given a yardstick. On that yardstick ten important words are printed for measuring. You may not be sure what to do with those yardsticks. Some of them have been laid on the table. What I want to ask all of you to do is to lay them out on the table so they point to the center like they are spokes on a wheel. What a grand picture that is creating! Now all of you are part of a new wheel.

Right now servers are waiting to serve. It's time to enjoy your banquet dinner!

When Steve came to the platform after dinner, he began by saying, "I want to ask you a question. 'How many of you are teachers?' I see a number of hands being lifted. But let me rephrase the question. 'How many of you are not teachers?'

You don't have to raise your hands.

I can answer that. All of you are teachers in some way.

In our history there is one iconic person who distinguished himself as a Teacher. That Teacher was skilled in refocusing big ideas down into simple phrases, like 'love your neighbor as yourself.' And, 'give and gifts will be given to you.' And, 'while you are knocking, the door will be opened.'

What if that Teacher's basic ideas can be refocused in ten words - ten universal qualities that we can use to measure who we are in our digital-information-molecular age? Those are the ten words printed on your yardsticks.

What if those ten words overarch all our varying religions, politics, and culture as universal identity markers? And, what if those words can be chosen by anyone, anywhere, at any time, as the identity markers that awaken our best dreams for our most successful life?

Now here's the test question. What if those words can be taught in all the learning centers of the world, especially to children? That was the far reaching dream of Dr. James Kelly. He is the central personality in the novel which extends his story through sequel books, with a comprehensive title of *A Place In The Story.*

One more what if question. What if you could be one of the special persons who gets to teach those words?

Before you begin to answer that, I want you to meet two very special persons who can help you see yourself in that picture.

Jenny Henderson, and Linda Kelly, would you please stand. Welcome them now with your enthusiastic applause!

Linda and Jenny, I already know how excited both of you are about this new venture where you will be training Big Ten Teachers. Linda, please come now and talk to us about this new far reaching idea!

Linda stepped to the center of the platform quickly and began by saying, "There are twenty-six letters in the ABC's alphabet and you learned them. They are basic in all our communications. There are ten words printed on your yardsticks. They are basic identity qualities for living your most successful life. And you can teach them!

Victor Hugo said, 'An invasion of armies can be resisted, but not an idea whose time has come." We sometimes revise that and say, 'nothing is as powerful as an idea whose time has come.' That is true of the Big Ten Universal Qualities. They are ten powerful words! Their time has come!

You were invited here this evening so you can be invited to be a part of a series of classes where these ten words are taught. It is an opportunity for you to be part of a commanding idea whose time has come!

All of you are invited to consider being a World Citizen Teacher. Don't let that idea scare you before you give yourself a chance to attend one of a series of classes where Jenny and I make it much like a game you can play. You can then find your ways to teach children how they can play the game as part of being a world citizen.

If you choose to be in one of our classes, you will be asked to read all of the *A Place In The Story* books. Dr. James Kelly is the wonderful granddad in all those books and you will have the privilege of learning about his positive, open-ended philosophy of life. As you read you will discover his dream that the Big Ten Universal Qualities be taught in all the learning centers of the world. And that's where you come on stage.

Do you think you could get five, six, ten or so children together so you could help them play a wonderful set of games in which they discover for themselves how these words can shape their best identity dreams? Could you invite them to your house for a series of game classes called a Big Ten World Citizen Class? Could you team up with a neighbor who might have a better place to meet? Could you get a Sunday school class to let you lead the class for about six sessions, or so, as an inserted unit, where they play this wonderful Big Ten Identity game? Could that be a part of a club children already belong to, like Boy Scouts or Girl Scouts. Could you get your little league coach to let you play these games with the team? On and on, there are many ways you could lead a group of children to begin this kind of identity discovery.

Jenny and I propose to teach you how to lead these games here at the center.

Here's one of the plans a teacher would use. You would be the leader of group of children, five or six, ten to fifteen. You would have ten four by six cards laid out on a table. Each card would have one of the Big Ten qualities printed in bold letters on it. On another table there would be many three by five cards laid out, each of which would have a word printed on it that could be matched up with one of the Big Ten words. A student would come and select one of the Big Ten words, and then take it over to the other table where there are many words, and choose one of those, then tell the class how or why the words are related. The Big Ten Words are KINDNESS, CARING, HONESTY, RESPECT, COLLABORATION, TOLERANCE, FAIRNESS, INTEGRITY, DIPLOMACY, NOBILITY. On the other table, with its three by five cards, there are many words, one word per card, from which to choose, like Considerate, Patience, Friendly, Honor, Worthy, Concern, Helpful, Flexible, Congenial, Joy, Smiles, Service, Forgiving, Esteem, Happiness, Confidence, Hero, Courtesy, Joy, Peace, Hope, Flexible, Giving, Inclusive, Networking, Cooperation Tactful, Humble, Courageous, Authentic, Disciplined, Generous, Visionary, Decisive, Latitude, Empathy, Confidence, Space, Adventurous, Appreciative, Tenacious, Integrity, Optimistic, Successful, Winners, Insightful, Dignity, Cordiality, Trust, Hopeful, Understanding, Oneness, Sharing, Buddies, Pal, Family, on and on - positive words that bear some connection to the Big Ten qualities.

Yes, of course, add other words that express qualities. And, yes, let students use their tablets or phones to help them in finding the meaning of words. And give the game a name which works for you, perhaps like MATCH-UP, or CONNECTIONS. It is an open-ended game that you can create new aspects of it as children play.

Then each child gets to tell why he or she chose their words. And you get to be the one who encourages them to share their ideas. You get to care and respect each child and his or her ideas, to be kind and understanding, to guide and nurture. You get to praise, compliment, and encourage. You get to bring out the best in each child. All the while the children get to enter into the conversation that follows and to build confidence as they both listen to others and develop their own associations. They all get into the game and help each other. It's so simple, but powerful.

As a teacher you can make sure each student gets to participate. Students will become more open, eager, and confident as they play. While they are playing the game, they will be awakening their most positive emotions, ideas, and identity. Hurts and fears will gradually turn into trust and hope. Measuring by the past will turn into measuring by the future, and new creative dreams. All this builds trust and social skills. Something gets healed and less defensive in their minds. And you become their trusted friend as a World Citizen Teacher.

When students play the game the first time they will be eager and ready to play it again. It's such a fun way to learn and develop healthy ideas, attitudes, and emotions that they will be ready to play it many times. You will watch them grow and find healing and wholeness – to move from conflict to unity. And, yes, you will grow also and find yourself interacting with your own most positive emotions and building your best dreams. All this time, they will be building a healthy positive identity!

After the children have explored these word associations they will be ready for the next game. And Jenny Henderson can tell you about that."

With equal enthusiasm, Jenny came and said, "This is a teaching skill I learned from another teacher. In a class of children, seated at a table or in a circle, the teacher has a sponge ball and tosses it to one of the children and says, 'Betty, tell me why kindness is such a bridge-building word.' While Betty holds the sponge ball she gets to express her understanding of that association, then tosses it back to the teacher. Then the teacher tosses it again and says, 'Larry, what makes the word, respect, such an important word at home.'

On and on the game proceeds. Be patient with each child. Give them time to express themselves. Let them sometimes pass the sponge ball to each other and interact together. Be very sensitive. So very quickly, this process can touch deep emotions, defenses, and fears, hopes and wishes. Don't rush the process, for in an instance, you may become an on-the-spot counselor. As the teacher, you will need to reach out to receive the sponge ball back at whatever point you see it is time to move one.

You are the guide. You can add and instruct. You can enter your own ideas and corrections. You can tell a story. You will have everyone's attention, especially when they wonder if they will be the next one to have the sponge ball tossed to them.

In an extended phase of the sponge ball session, you can lead into another time when you ask students to put the Big Ten words into sentences. You may ask each student to write a story of five to ten sentences. Then each student will be given a chance to read his or her story to the class. This may develop into such a group-centered activity that you can ask them to sit in groups of three or four and work together to write a story. Start the story off by saying, let your story begin with, 'When Bobbie got home from school....' All the while, you are the teacher and are dealing with identity and creative emotions.

Perfection in writing a story is not the name of the game, it's association, guiding, nurturing, expanding ideas, guiding students to care about and respect the ideas of others, learning and using positive emotions and related ideas. Be creative. There are many ways of leading your class. Two of you may team up together to lead a class.

Depending on the level of your students and the level of interest and participation, a teacher may choose to read the Joseph story that is in the *Apple Blossom Time* book aloud to students. A teacher may choose to read Ben Daniel's lawnmower story in the individual book, *A Place In The Story*.

There are other stories or sections from any of the books about Dr. Kelly that a teacher may chose to read. You may choose to read the Ten Principles of Problem Solving from *The Future We Ask For*. Be creative and open. Care and share. Learn as you go, and go as you learn.

If you feel your class has grown to a new level, it may be time to ask them to write new positive proverbs on 4 x 6 cards. You may be pleasantly surprised at how good some of these proverbs may be.

If your class is with youth or adults, you may ask them to write some positive affirmations of faith.

Your guidance of this dynamic will be best when you incorporate the very positive philosophy you acquired as you read all of the books in *A Place In The Story*. Your reading can help you share a faith, confidence, and understanding that is big and overarching so both you and your students develop an identity that is inclusive and healthy.

At the same time that you are a part of the Big Ten Teachers training classes, you may have overlapping roles as a professional teacher, a loving parent, a friend, a community leader, an uncle, aunt, grandparent, and especially as a friend, linked together to work upstream to help students grow and develop their best qualities into their identity.

What we want is not to achieve perfection in teaching but lots of caring so you are helping make a better tomorrow for each student by silently working upstream.

The dream gets bigger. Beyond the World Citizen Center here, there can be parallels to what we have created here. The ongoing dream is that World Citizen Teachers across the world will create their own parallel to a world citizen center and begin to new wave of classes that train teachers to become World Citizen Teachers! A bold dream? Yes. But, possible? Yes!

But for here and now, this is your time to be a part of an idea whose time has come. Can you see yourself being a part of this kind of dream for new tomorrows in the world family?

And now, Linda, as though the sponge ball is passed back to you, would you share your story here at this banquet occasion about why you have such a passion for teaching teachers to become Big Ten Teachers."

Linda began thoughtfully. "That began to be a part of my identity when I sat on Granddad's farmhouse porch and heard him tell stories about people who needed to find their own best dreams for new tomorrows. And when Granddad told his dream about having the Big Ten Universal Qualities taught in all the learning centers of the world, I knew he was passing that dream torch on to me. I knew that I needed to be that kind of teacher. So when I was told about this new program here at the World Citizen Center, I knew I wanted to be a part of it.

Jenny and I want all of you to be one of those leaders who is working upstream as a Big Ten Teacher. We want to encourage you to catch the torch and become a teacher in one of the world's centers of learning. You can be a World Citizen Teacher!

And now, Steve, over to you."

"Thank you, Linda! And thank you, Jenny! This is a great opportunity for anyone who chooses to be in one of these classes!

Now as for the classes Linda and Jenny will be leading here at the World Citizen Center for teachers, the hope is that many people will take the classes and then find ways they can launch their own Big Ten World Citizen Classes for children.

No, you don't have to become a teacher to be in these classes. Anyone can be a part of these classes. But the overall instructions will be focused on helping you to become a teacher. And for those who complete the classes, we will encourage you to be creative and invent places where you can be a teacher - at home, in the community, school, Sunday school, youth group, club, or where a group of you decide to meet in each others homes and take turns leading one of the classes.

So with adaptation, these classes can be for youth or adults. Some of you may be in leadership at planning retreats where fellow workers search for an identity above and beyond career planning and job performance, where the goal is to develop new skills in human relations under the umbrella of an overarching identity defined by the ten universal qualities. It's all open-ended. And, yes, you can play the word game and the sponge ball game in adult sessions. You will be amazed at the level of insight and crossover ideas these will awaken and release. It's a kind of blanket invitation. The goal is that many of you will say, 'yes I want to be a teacher,' or just be in one of these classes.

One year from now we will have a Celebration Banquet when we will have gathered lots of anecdotal stories about how you have become World Citizen Teachers, or have experienced significant positive change from being a part of these classes. It will be a celebration banquet for those who have been in these classes, or have taught their own classes, to share stories that tell what a difference for good these classes have made.

Now, with the imaginary sponge ball now in my hand, I sense that it is time to give you an opportunity to respond.

The first step is for you to come to the front where we have request forms that you can fill out to indicate your desire to be a part of these classes. Then we will work out a time you can be one of those who gets to take these wonderful classes.

The second step is to get into one of the Big Ten Teacher classes as a learner of the Big Ten Universal Qualities.

The third step then would be to purchase and read the books that tell Dr. James Kelly's story and philosophy of life, as you participate in the classes.

As a follow-up you can consider being a teacher, now that you have had training as a World Citizen Teacher.

Then if, upon completion of the classes, you choose to be a World Citizen Teacher, you will be certified and given a Gold Yardstick!

It's an opportunity whose time has come.

As we close this event, if you don't have a Big Ten yardstick, there people standing at the door ready to give you a yardstick so we may all go out into life as a successful person who measures by the Big Ten Universal Qualities.

CHAPTER EIGHT

Daybreak on the Mountain

IT WAS CELEBRATION TIME FOR CLARK AND JENNY, BRIAN AND LINDA, Steve and Sandra. Dr. Logan had invited them to come up to Eagles View Mountain for breakfast and to be there early, in time for daybreak.

After more wood had been put on the fire in the fireplace and the breakfast dishes had been put away, with all of them helping, Dr. Logan asked all his colleagues to look to the east. "It's daybreak," he said. "I have celebrated daybreak up here many times, but none more special than this. Right now the sun is peeking up over the mountains on the eastern side of Alpine and we can begin to see the World Citizen Center in the dim light of dawn down there.

What a privilege we now share. I wanted you to come up here in this early morning hour so we could share the perspective of where we are in an almost unbelievable story. It's a kind of celebration moment for all of us.

I want you to know how privileged I am to have a part in this almost unbelievable story. But all of us have a privileged place in this story.

We know Clark and Jenny have a story about the time they came back out to the apple farm, following the passing of Clark's parents. Brian and Jenny's story reaches back to Dr. Kelly's farmhouse porch. Steve and Sandra have a story that has opened up in special ways right here in Alpine. And I have my own parallel story that I want to share that celebrates the stewardship of my parents.

After my parents died that left me in charge of their estate and lots of money. They had accumulated resources out of several business ventures and investments. I was the sole beneficiary.

What could I do with those resources? I didn't need the money. I had my own career as a professor. I already had what I needed for a good life. So I asked our family lawyer to sweep the majority of the estate resources together and turn them into an endowment that I called Vision Foundation.

Vision for what? I waited and thought about things I could support. I read Dr. James Kelly's books and waited. Then it began to come together. Out of deep disappointment with a church I attended one Sunday, I set up an appointment with Sandra, and later with Steve, at the World Citizen Church. I had read in Dr. Kelly's books about Center Church and how the people there turned what was their large fellowship hall into a conference center, then out of the success of that, they expanded it into a state of the art grand conference center. My question to Sandra as minister of World

Citizen Church was, 'why can't we create a conference center like that here as a part of our church?' That question became a dream we explored and something I could support with my Vision Foundation. Hence, as we look down over Alpine, we can see the World Citizen Center. And the dream goes on. It's growing. Clark and Jenny, Linda and Brian have now become a part of the dream.

I attended our first Yardstick Success Rally and was immensely pleased. Then I came to the World Citizen Teachers Banquet and could hardly believe all this had once been only a dream. Could this be real? I was delighted. It was real. I often think of that two word paradigm, 'Noblesse oblige'. Nobility obligates. Privilege equals privilege. What a privilege we all have to be a part of this. It's a daybreak celebration!

So, tell us, Steve, what do you think? Since I called for this daybreak session, I get to ask the question. Steve, what do you think? Where are we?"

A moment of silence indicated that Steve was not going to give a casual answer. "I am pleased that you have shared the part your parents have played in all this. I already knew much of your story, but never saw it in the perspective of this daybreak meeting up here. So, thank you so much for inviting all of us up here for this special early six o'clock celebration breakfast.

We could have met in the Eagles View Conference Room and just looked up here but that would not have equaled this perspective. Up here, and down there, are connected by a big bold dream.

I look around this table and see the leaders who launched both the Big Ten Success Rally and the World Citizen Teachers program and realize how fortunate we are to have Clark and Jenny

Henderson, and Brian and Linda Kelly on this team of daring dreamers.

And, David, I realize anew how much we are indebted to your parents that enabled you to create the Vision Foundation as a way to support this great venture cause at this strategic time. And all of us owe a special thanks to Sandra as a leader of the forward thinking people of World Citizen Church. Can you believe how incredibly unique that church is? I see that more clearly than ever now. That first Sunday when I was up here and decided to drive down into Alpine and to the World Citizen Church, I walked into a church where its people were ready to invest in new tomorrows. Right now, if I had a yardstick, I would raise it in a high salute to all of you!

So, let me stop here and give the rest of you an opportunity to share your perspective on our little daybreak celebration up here. Clark, would you like to lead the way?"

Clark responded, "I would be pleased to share my views. But even more I sense that all of us would like to hear Dr. Logan talk about how the *A Place In The Story* books keep leading our story. Dr. Logan could you tell us more?"

David began quietly and reflectively. "I don't want people to know very much about how much money I put into this through the foundation. They can guess that it was more than a couple dollars.

I believe we are stewards of the resources put into our hands, and that is never just a matter of money, it's a matter of dreams and vision and what we can do to advance our humanity to higher levels. To me, that's sacred. So, it's not that building down there

or the money, but the dreams we advance in our story, that's what
is important. As for the money, I believe in what we are doing
and am ready to put in more. And behind the scenes, the World
Citizen Center has created its own foundation to make sure we
don't get the jitters in testing moments. We are engaged in the
cause of helping people to be successful in their life, and that's not
just about money. It's about identity. It's about the qualities we live
by. Quietly, I want to stand behind this dream that is in progress.

Now, don't you dare come to me and thank me for what I am
doing. It's a stewardship of the gifts put into my care. It's a stewardship of identity and dreams that is important."

When Dr. Logan stopped speaking, Steve asked, "Does anyone
else have something they would like to add?"

Linda spoke up quietly and said, "I know you have heard about
my special moment before. But my thoughts go back to that time
we nine grandchildren sat on the farmhouse porch following the
memorial service for Granddad. It was a sacred and defining moment. I think all of us sensed that Granddad had passed the flaming
touch of dreams down to his beloved grandchildren. I don't know
how many felt they were supposed to catch that touch, I just know
I was supposed to catch it. From the perspective of his moment I
now believe that in some way all of us here have caught that torch."

"Well," Dr Logan said, "Daybreak has already turned into
sunrise and the sun is half way up the sky now. But let me add a
little more.

We know that the qualities defining our identity in the Big
Ten really and truly do work. In ways which keep opening up,
they help us to dream big. As we dream, we know these qualities

can never be mandated across the world. They have to be chosen. And for them to be chosen they need to be taught. And, for that to happen we must never let go of the dream that they be taught in all the learning places of the world.

That's our dream here at the World Citizen Center, and that's our mission.

What a high privilege we all share in a stewardship of dreams. Let's keep it going! Let's give away as many yardsticks as we can!"

CHAPTER NINE

The Gold Yardstick Celebration Banquet

"WELCOME TO THE GOLD YARDSTICK CELEBRATION BANQUET!" Linda said with excitement. "I, along with my co-teacher in the Big Ten World Citizen Teachers program, Jenny Henderson, welcome you to this celebration banquet. When this special program was launched we announced then that we would celebrate with those who completed their training one year from that time. Now here we are. You were told you would be given a Gold Big Ten Yardstick to celebrate your completing the course as a teacher. I know there are many of you here who have your Gold Yardstick. You did what you were asked to do, bring them to the banquet. It's show time. Would you pick up your Gold Big Ten Yardsticks and wave them in the air as a celebration of one year of pioneering success.

We all love to hear good stories. This year of pioneering new-ness has resulted in many great stories, so many, in fact that it was not easy to choose which ones to share with you. We will hear some of those success stories after we have enjoyed a great banquet dinner together. Our servers are standing by just waiting for a sig-nal to begin. Servers, you may begin now!"

Following the banquet dinner, Linda came back to the plat-form. "What a privilege it is for me to be here with you. When Brian and I first came to Alpine and stood in the parking lot, looking up at the World Citizen Center, we were awed by its mag-nificence. But it is being here tonight with you that lets me see its real significance. You are the ones who have made dreams become real. I celebrate with you the loyalty and devotion so many have given to bring us to this Big Ten World Citizen Teachers Banquet.

What I want to do now is to ask my colleague in teaching, Jenny Henderson, to come now to greet you and introduce the program."

"Good evening!" Jenny Henderson said as soon as she got to the platform. "Along with you, I am looking forward to this story time. There are ten people out there among you who will come and tell you their story. In our early planning time we were asking, 'How can we get people to come to this banquet?' That was a mute question. The question became, 'How can we limit the number we can invite so we do not overrun our seating capacity?'

So many of you have been in our success rallies and teacher training classes. Out there among you are ten people who have been invited to come and occupy the ten empty chairs up here, and tell us their story."

From all across the banquet hall people made their way to the platform and sat down.

When they were seated, Jenny said, "This is story time. These are among many people who responded with an invitation to put their story down in around two hundred words. From that deluge of stories, we selected stories that represent a wide spectrum of viewpoints. That was not easy, given how many great stories were sent in. Ten have been selected. These ten are now asked to come to the center of the platform and tell you their stories without any introduction from me. One by one they will get up and tell you their story. We drew numbers to see who would be number one, two, three on down to number ten. So let's begin with number one."

Veranda walked to the center and began thoughtfully. "Three years ago I hit a big snag in my life and in my thinking. I mean big. During that time of struggle I heard about the Yardstick Success Rally. I went to that rally. I heard the speakers. I purchased the books. I read them. Did I ever read them - my name was written all through the stories. Not really, of course, but I was in those stories. I was one of those people caught in an old ending who needed a new beginning.

I was one of those privileged to attend the classes. At home, I looked at my yardstick as I kept reading Dr Kelly's books, hoping that the secret to my new beginning was in those ten words. Timid and insecure me, I kept quiet about the fact that I was searching for a way to reset my identity as I measured by those ten words.

But my parents noticed a change. And, I felt the change inside. Then one day my employer said, 'Veranda, what's happened to you? You've changed.' I hardly knew what to say. But I admitted that I had been reading a set of books called, *A Place In The Story.* When I asked him if he had ever heard of those books, he said, 'No.' Cautiously I asked, 'Would you like to read them if I loaned them to you?'

He said, 'If that is the way to find out what's happened, yes, I would read them.' Well, he read them. And, we met to talk about them. And guess what. It wasn't long before he asked me something. He said, 'Veranda, would you marry me?' And guess what I said."

Someone from the audience spoke up loudly and said with enthusiasm, "You said, 'Yes!'

"You are right. That's what I said. That's not a newspaper headlines story, but that's my story, and I'm sticking to it. And to him. So, that's not just my story, it's our story. I still have my Gold Yardstick, and we are beginning our marriage measuring by those ten words!"

Veranda sat down while the audience was still applauding.

When the second speaker got up he said, "Well, I certainly don't have a story to match that. So I will just tell my own less than spectacular story. It's one that is very real for me. I was wounded in Iraq. You saw me walk up here and may not have noticed anything different about me. But there was a difference.

I was at the first Yardstick Success Rally in a wheel chair, because a friend wouldn't let me alone until I agreed to go with him to the rally. He came to the hospital and got me. There was nothing any speaker said about amputees. But there was that one word a speaker used, that phrase, Noblesse oblige. Nobility obligates. Privilege obligates. Privilege? I didn't have privilege. I had been stripped of privilege. But I accepted one of the yardsticks they were giving away and brought it back to the hospital. Other veterans asked me about the yardstick. My answers were limp and devoid of any expectation that those words applied to me. It took time. That yardstick kept leaning up against my bed. I picked it up and handled it gently, like a kid would handle a treasured little baseball. Gradually my thinking changed. Finally I asked the chaplain about the, *A Place In The Story,* books and he said he would get me a set, or that I could just wheel down to the library - that they had the full set there. I went to the library immediately. I read about turning closed gates behind me into open gates before me. Gradually the depression and despair turned into hope. I went to therapy with a new identity. I could plant a new garden. I know, it's all metaphor, but I made it a metaphor for me. I got a prosthesis. I got a job. My home became a home again. The healing was in my mind, in my identity. I know, there are lots of stories like this. Many of my comrades made a far bigger sacrifice than I, and some made the ultimate sacrifice. But we knew in those critical moments, even in the tragedies of war, we were engaged in the march of freedom and hope. I began to realize I was still engaged in the march of hope. I knew that I needed to move forward and help build a world that is better and free of the tragedies of war. I wanted a healing that helped the human family to find a new age of oneness in the world. We are not there yet. Will we ever be? I don't know, but in some way I want to be a part of that possibility. So that's my story and my place in a bigger story. So I proudly stand here before you with my prosthesis."

When he pulled up his pants to show his prosthesis, the audience stood in a celebrating applause of respect.

Speaker number three got up. On the way to the center, he turned and shook hands with the amputee as he returned to his seat.

"They asked me just to tell my story. It's not as dramatic as the two you have already heard. I was a minister who went to that Yardstick Success Rally in my city. I was a very negative minister. I had my own version of Paul on the road to Damascus. I didn't have a faith, I had a theology which I, like Paul, defended harshly. It was as rigid as Paul's was before his Damascus Road. I was locked in the past. In that view of the Bible, every word was literally true. I defended that view tenaciously, as though it were something sacred. Shall I say it, I was heartless toward people who had different views. In spite of all that, I bought those books they had for sale at the rally and brought them home and began to read the first book, where the granddad in the story, told Paul's story. It was my story. I saw myself. Like Paul, I had a religion, but not a faith. I discovered a new image for myself. My thinking changed. I took that word, kindness, to heart and started being kind to everyone I met, no matter what their theological views were. It was like Dr. Kelly said, the word, kindness, was a magic word. I began to live out Paul's description of a changed man. I became a new man in Christ, not in theology, or comparison to, or in contrast to, some other religion, but as a faith that was big, open, and caring. I was on my own Damascus Road.

Now that yardstick is proudly displayed in my study, and I hope those ten words are reflected in my preaching and in all my ministry. So, what do I do? I give yardsticks away. Just ask me for one. I have a lot of them. I would like other people to have one, people who need a Damascus Road of their own."

The next speaker didn't wait until he got to the center to begin talking with excitement.

"Books. Books have change my life. As a psychiatrist one has to read a lot of books on the way to a degree. So many good books are written by good people and that's the best part of it. One gets to know some of the greatest people of all time through their books.

So, I have met Dr. James Kelly through his books.

There is another special person I have meet through her book, Dr. Carol S. Dweck. Her book is called, *Mindset*. Dr. Dweck thinks like I think, or maybe, I should say I think like she thinks. Her thesis is that the way you think about yourself can actually reset your life so that you become that person you see yourself being. That person is not measured by who you have been, so much as by who you see yourself becoming with an open, positive growth mindset.

Input your mind with a new sense of possibilities and that lifts your story to a new level. It becomes a positive identity mindset.

I know someone else who thinks like that? It's Dr. Norman Doidge. That's the premise of his book, *The Mind That Changes Itself*. His premise is that the brain is plastic and rewrites itself so it becomes a guiding and leading inner influence.

I know another writer who understands that. It's Dr. Martin E. P. Selegman. He wants us to be optimistic and concentrate on our signature strengths, as a way to guide us beyond our weaknesses. No wonder one of his books is called, *Authentic Happiness*.

So, do you wonder that I like Dr. James Kelly's writings and wanted to take a class where his Big Ten words are taught as a way of shaping one's life for new tomorrows? No, you don't wonder about that, because you understand that the Big Ten words are power words that can add significantly to your strengths.

Imagine this. There I was, a psychiatrist, sitting in a class with teachers and parents who want to learn how to teach the ten words to children. And me, sitting there thinking the same thing, that I want to teach these ten words to children. How did that turn out? Well, I have my gold yardstick and proud to be among the certified World Citizen Teachers. I am planning to get a class together, but not for children. I want to have a class for parents of children, which in turn, will of course also be for children. Parents are the ones who need to be challenged by the ten words. If they will live by those words they will be better parents and their children will be more successful people. So, does it make a difference if parents define who they are by high standards, and live that out before their children?

I don't have a class yet, but I have my gold yardstick and am ready to sign up ten parents here tonight - five couples who might want to be in my class.

Five couples? Just ten people? Yes. Five couples, so we can meet in each others homes and get to know each other where parenting takes place. Will my wife be with me? When I asked her she enthusiastically said, 'Of course. We are parents and we are a team.'

When I get that class together, we will be networking with each other as fellow parents in a teaching-learning quest. I am confident that, if those of us who are parents will make the big ten words a part of our identity vocabulary, we will be better parents and our children will be better children. Parents need an identity reset, especially when it is reset by the Big Ten qualities. So talk to me. Tonight. I am ready to start a class and learn along with you."

The next speaker walked over slowly and thoughtfully. "This is hard," she began. "Not just to stand before people and talk, I do that day by day. I am a teacher. But I am also a mother and wife, and we lost our little four year old boy to leukemia. That was hard. It still hurts now, three years later. There were times when I went into meltdowns and just broke down and cried.

Yes, my husband and I went to grief counseling sessions. That helped. What also has helped is to remember that the people at the children's hospital were so great. They were angels. Talk about kindness and caring - they lived it in their professions. They did all they could. And people raised money to help cover additional costs. That helped too.

But what helped so much was to keep repeating a line from Dr. Kelly in which he says, 'you can't take hold of the future unless you turn loose of the past.' I also locked onto the advice Paul gave to his friends at Philippi. It runs a close parallel to the Big Ten qualities we can choose for healing thoughts. Paul's advice was that we should choose our thoughts - select the ones that are positive and give uplift, like focusing on what is true and good, pure and lovely. We are advised to think about the fine and good things in other people, like what I said about the angels at the children's hospital. Paul's summation was to think all we can be glad about. I knew I still had so much to be glad about and that it was up to me to think about that.

When I heard about the Big Ten World Citizen Teachers program I knew it was something I wanted to be a part of and learn how I could share my insights. I want to help others. So I have my gold yardstick.

What I am so aware of now is that all any of us have is a place

in the story. All our little boy had was a place in the story. He
didn't choose it, and I didn't choose it. What I could choose was
to make the best of un-chosen places. And that's what I have, a
place in the story which honors the lessons learned in sorrow.
In that story, two words stand our. Kindness and respect. I am
grateful for the kind and caring people that I have come to know.
And I have a new respect for medical science and what is being
done in research.

But what I also have now is respect for the nature of existence.
No one lives forever. All we ever get, no matter who we are, is a
niche in a bigger story. Long or short, that's the nature of human
consciousness. Beyond that, we become a part of the mystery of
all molecular existence.

May I be openly honest with you. It seems strange to talk about
the shortness of life - that when it's over, it's over, but that paradigm also gives me comfort. People talk to me and say, 'Jason is in
a better place.' I stumble a moment. Better place? You just don't
know how empty that sounds unless you've lost a close member of
your family. It's consoling to know that the story has an end - that
it can be over - that it doesn't have to go on in an endless state
of being some kind of spirit, living somewhere out there with no
more meaning than just existing forever, without purpose or plan.

So I have respect for an awareness that all we ever get is our
little niche in the story, where hard as it is, we have to put the past
behind us so we can do what we can to turn old endings into new
beginnings.

One part of my new beginning is to have become a Big Ten
World Citizen Teacher in a Sunday School Class, where I not only
teach, but am learning to measure by all the Big Ten qualities that

begins with kindness. The story goes on, of course, where what we plan to give to life becomes our request of life."

As she turned to go back to her seat there was a moment of deep silence. Then, one by one people began to stand quietly, in a tribute of caring and respect."

Steve walked on stage and paused. "These stories are wonderful. But we need to be aware of the time frame. So, let's take five minutes to stand up and stretch. But don't you dare go anywhere unless. Well, unless."

CHAPTER TEN

The Gold Yardstick Celebration Banquet Continued

THE NEXT SPEAKER BEGAN SPEAKING JUST AS SOON AS SHE STOOD, THEN gestured toward her fellow speakers and said, "So far, we are all reading from the same page. We are all talking about, who we are, and who we want to be." She walked to the center and said, "I want to talk about the ten identity words we can choose for our story.

Someone said that, more significant than going to the moon is the realization that we self-create by the input we give to our brain. We are molecular, but we are much more than that. We are people. We have brains. And our brain works for us. So much of what we are and what we do, is written into our DNA. But what is also written there is the ability to input the brain so it becomes our self-directed guide, a kind of preset or default that makes us goal directed. Our mind becomes magnetized and we are attracted to ideas and things that help us to become that person we input to the brain. So it is of highest importance is that we ask our brain to guide us to the best we can be.

You may have guessed it. I teach philosophy in college. I am dealing with the plasticity of our brain. Dr. Norman Doidge and Dr. James Kelly both talk about how the brain changes itself by the identity markers we feed into it.

I don't need to say more than what has already been said by the speakers who have already talked about new ways of thinking. It is a gift of our DNA that is to be highly respected - we have choices. One choice I will make is to make space in my classes for a segment of sessions in which I share my Big Ten journey with my students.

Now, I want to make an assumption at this point, and that is, that you had rather hear what this twelve-year-old boy sitting beside me has to say than to hear what else I could say. So, my young friend, I am ready to sit down so you can stand up and share your story.

"Already?" he said as a kind of question, as he got up, and haltingly started to the center. "I thought I had more time to be nervous. Anyway, here's my story.

My fifth grade teacher attended the World Citizen Teachers class here and has adopted a teaching skill of one of the teachers used. So in class one day, right out of the clear, my teacher threw the sponge ball to me and said, 'Kenny, what are you learning in our class?' I didn't speak up quickly, so she put out her hands, ready for me to return the ball. But I kept the ball, and quickly said, 'Confidence. That's what I am learning. Confidence. And I need a big shot of it right now.' Everyone in the class laughed in a kind of 'me too' chuckle.

So I tossed the sponge ball back to her. She caught it and was about to toss it to someone else, but she tossed it right back to me and said, 'Tell the class a story that illustrates confidence.'

I hadn't expected that so I had to think fast. I muscled up my confidence and said, 'In the third grade I was part of a little ball team. I wasn't the best player, so when it came my turn to go to bat, I already knew I would strike out. I had done it too many times before. I made an assumption that it would happen again. I walked over to the plate timidly and waited. That's when the coach said, 'Time.' He came over and talked to me. He said, 'How many possibilities will that pitcher give you to hit at a ball?'

I figured a moment and said, 'Well, I get three strikes. Is that what you mean?'

'That's it. Now, pick a good one and give it everything you've got!'

I did! Then the next thing I realized was that I also needed to run with all the speed I had to first base. What I learned was that I needed to match the pitcher's confidence that he could strike me out, with the confidence that I could show him he couldn't. And when I gave it all I had, confidence won.

Out of that I began to pick some new friends, other students who had confidence. I even gained the confidence that I could get up here and speak. If I keep going in the direction I have started I believe I can be a successful person."

Somewhat surprised at himself, Kenny turned and looked out into the audience and said, "Coach. Dad. Thanks! And my fifth grade teacher, I know you are out there too. Thanks! Could all the rest of you help me and give both of them a big hand?"

It was a surprise ending for the audience and they began applauding all three of them, the boy, the teacher, and his dad!

The next speaker got up and said, "There's a kind of theme running through our speeches, and what I have to say may have crossover parallels. In college I learned to be a good student. I wasn't that way in high school where I was mostly a B student, but in college I gave myself a new identity. It wasn't spelled out - it was just an 'I can.' approach. I learned to give my best to my studies. After college, I got my Masters degree and then my Ph D. Then I went into research, where my special interest revolves around regenerative medicine. I benefit from those who have special knowledge and skills in many fields of medicine. I know enough about crossovers to know I need to network with others. So I lead a research team which is searching for ways to replace failing parts in our bodies.

So, what if we get really good at this and replace failing organs so that we live a long time? The front cover on one issue of Time Magazine showed a baby's picture and then had a caption that said, "This baby could live to be 142 years old." That's not forever, but much longer than now. How does that change what's important and who we choose to be for our identity markers? That has become of major interest to me now that we are working on replacement for failed body parts. The lines are blending between science, the humanities, faith and philosophy, and more and more I have been looking for answers to the big questions about who we are in an age when we have increasing potential to self design and change our story. While I was in the Big Ten World Citizen classes I decided I wanted to find a way to be one of the Gold Yardstick Teachers. I haven't found it yet, but I will.

Some quickly assume these qualities cannot be taught. I am confident that just the opposite is true, and that not only can they be taught, they need to be taught extensively in an age when our potential to self design is increasing rapidly. So my open question I deal with in my research is not just, how can we extend length of life, but how can we enhance quality of life. I want to make my research explore ways to live, not just longer, but better. I think the Big Ten Universal Qualities can help us define more wholesome ways to live so we make wise choices in our relationships with each other in the world family.

Wiser. That's what I want, wise enough to choose to be big minded and big hearted, to be tolerant, and fair. I want us to have integrity with the expanding knowledge base of our time. And I want us to learn to collaborate as never before so that the engineers and chemists, and physicists, and all the sciences, work together so that the end game is to help us to keep rising to a higher humanity. This way the old advertising slogan is not only 'better science for better living,' but 'better identity for better quality living.' That's our challenge-opportunity in our time in history. I like being a part of what's happening here at our World Citizen Center!"

A distinguished man with white hair came to the center and paused. His manner indicated that he would be thoughtful in what he had to say. "There is one more speaker after me. I am looking forward to her story. As for my story, my association with the

World Citizen Center is very recent. As I have listened to the stories being told here tonight, I am convinced that a recent decision I made is right, so right, that I am ready to share it.

Two weeks ago I called Dr. Sandra at her office at the church and asked if she could set up a meeting so I could talk with her and Steve.

When I arrived and went in, Dr. Sandra asked if I would like a cup of coffee. I said, 'Yes. And I would like for you and Steve to join me so it will seem like we are friends just sitting down to visit.' Actually it was more than that. So, while we were sipping our coffee. I sat my cup on the table and said, 'Dr. Sandra, I have been a member of this church for many years. You have been among its very best ministers. No, no, I am not trying to flatter you. From my point of view, that is very true. My years are getting fewer and fewer now. You will be the one who will have my memorial service because I have a sickness that will take me away soon. I wanted both you and Steve to know how I am looking at things from that perspective and a longer view of how to make my story count.

I remember, soon after you came here, Dr. Sandra, that some of us began to think that the name of our church no longer defined who we were. The name, Grovemont Church, suggested that we were just a church, tucked away in the little mountain town of Alpine, set to serve our little niche here in the valley. Dr. Sandra, you began to talk like we had a mission to live by a bigger understanding of our faith - that if we lived by our best qualities there were no boundaries to our place in the human story, that, like Jesus, we were on a mission to serve humanity. You said that wherever we lived and served, those qualities made us world citizens. You had no idea of the scope of what you had said, but in that phrase, world citizens, you were renaming this church. It focused the way some of us were thinking. So we brought a proposal to the church council that we rename our church, World Citizen Church.

Then when you and Dr. David Logan brought your ideas to the council about having a center that would align the concept of world citizens into a conference center, we knew it was part of who we were trying to be. We adopted the proposal that we create the World Citizen Center as an adjacent, but separate, part of that mission. I voted in favor of it and take pride in that vote. I believe in what we are doing here. It's a mission, but it's more than that. It's a cause. It's a cause that calls us to give our best to make the human story the best it has ever been. And I have never believed it more than tonight, as I sat here listening to these stories.

I have talked to my personal lawyer and asked him to take care of my plans for my estate. I told him that I have no family and that after all expenses are taken care of, I want the remainder of my estate to go to the World Citizen Center Foundation.'

I am very reluctant to tell about this, but that's what I told Sandra and Steve that day at the church, so I am telling it now as a way to add my story to the World Citizen Center story. I may be here a while yet, who knows, but plans for my estate are in place now and I feel confident about that. It's all set up. I believe one of the responsibilities we have for our story is to make sure we try to support some of the human family's great causes. The World Citizen Center and its program is a great cause and I am pleased to have some part in its future.

And that's what I wanted to say. I want no thanks. No praise. It's just that I am privileged to say it here among people who are making the dream of the World Citizen Center come alive and go forward. I am glad I can have a part of it."

A respectful quietness followed. Then one person stood up and began a hushed applause that spread until everyone was standing in mutual respect.

The last speaker was obviously in her young adult years. Actually she had just finished her teaching degree and was in her first year of teaching. "I am one of the teachers with a gold yardstick," she said. "I am proud of it. It's kind of like a Master's degree in new dreams for service. It's a distinction that I share with so many of you here. We are colleagues. We have a "Gold Yardstick Degree."

What I want to do at this point in my career is to have units in each semester of my school year in which I teach the Big Ten Universal Qualities to my students. Since these are basic human qualities that overarch religion, politics, and culture there can be no conflict. Beyond that I want to explore ways that teaching the Big Ten can become a part of college curriculum, so that all teachers with a degree in Education will have a chance to do what I am doing wherever they teach.

Beyond that, what I celebrate so much is that this program includes the recognition that parents need to be schooled in the Big Ten Universal Qualities. In whatever their housing may be like, a house, a mobile home, an apartment, or castle, parents are in one of the most important learning places in all the world.

So, yes, I have big dreams. I want to link up with my church to provide a class in the Big Ten for parents and teach it at least twice a year. So, I am taking a big step here tonight? Yes. I have talked

with Dr Sandra and to the church school coordinator at our World
Citizen Church and we will begin those classes this summer. I don't
have much else to say other than to admit that I am as green as a
gourd and as daring as a chicken, and ready to jump in the water
with both feet, and do what I can to be a world citizen wherever
I am. How's that for mixed metaphors?

So, at the end of this banquet, no matter what church you attend, or no church, come up and talk to me. Let's keep this kind
of dream going."

Steve walked on stage quickly and said, "If you ever wanted
to stand to celebrate at the end of a great speech, my guess is that
you want to stand now at the end of ten great speeches! Let's do
it together!

Amid thunderous applause by a grateful standing audience,
Steve waited and then motioned for them to be seated again.

"What else needs to be said?" Steve said. "Not much. If we
embrace the qualities of the Big Ten for our future identity, we can
look back and wish we had built these qualities into our oneness
identity years, decades, and centuries earlier. While we cannot
change the past, we can move forward into the future with bold
dreams. This is our time to get as close as we can to great utopian
dreams.

I like to refer to the Bill and Melinda Gates and their work
through their foundation. Melinda says, 'we always try to work
upstream.'

Work upstream. Those two words focus what we are trying
to do in new ways to make sure the Big Ten Universal Qualities

are taught in all the learning centers of the world. We have made a daring, bold, new upstream beginning here tonight.

What time is it? Time to close out our wonderful banquet? Yes. But beyond that, it is time to take up our yardsticks and honor the new sacred in our sunrise dream for new tomorrows!

"Your ticket to this banquet was to bring your yardstick. Could we all now lift our yardsticks high in a salute to new tomorrows, saying, the Big Ten for New Tomorrows. Let's say it together, THE BIG TEN FOR NEW TOMORROWS!

CHAPTER ELEVEN

What If ?

THE SUNDAY MORNING WORSHIP SERVICE AT WORLD CITIZEN Church had come to that point which was a highlight for many people, the sermon. As Dr. Sandra stood at the pulpit, she said, "This is Earth Sunday. For many years we have focused on the environment and the responsibility we have for our biosphere, Earth. At times we have invited guest speakers whose studies and experience made them specialist, with a knowledge base that could help us define our place in an environmental world view.

When I began to think about a guest speaker for Earth Sunday this year, I began to think about persons who would bring us new and helpful insights for understanding our place in the earth story. That's when I had an, aha moment, and said to myself, 'we have that person right here in Alpine!' My guess is that some of you may be thinking of the same person I thought about in my moment of insight.

That person came here to write his dissertation on environmental science and moved into Dr. David Logan's, Look Beyond, cottage up on Eagles View Mountain for the summer. He was only going to be there for that summer, but as ideas and events came together in surprising ways he stayed longer than that summer and has now become the Director of the World Citizen Center. You know that story and you know who I am talking about. And you know that he is an environmental scientist and one of the best speakers we could find anywhere to be our guest speaker for Earth Sunday. He is so well known and respected that he needs little introduction. But then, I could proudly tell you, he is my husband. But you already know that. You may remember that our wedding was right here in this church, and that our wedding ceremony was led by his distinguished granddad, Dr. James Kelly, whose writings inspired the beginning of the World Citizen Center. That center is a vital part of this church. And it's new director is well known in all of Alpine. He is our guest speaker today. So, I now present to you, Dr. Steve Kelly."

Steve moved to the pulpit as if he were eager to speak. He began immediately by saying, "What a surprising and wonderful journey it has been since I came here. I came to Alpine to do research and writing. I was privileged to live in Dr. David Logan's retreat house high up on Eagles View Mountain. What I didn't know then was that I had moved into a special environment, not just the wonderful climate up on the mountain, or down here in this thermal belt in Alpine, but into an environment of big, bold, ideas and dreams.

I discovered that special environment on that first Sunday morning when I decided to come down the mountain to this church. I was cordially received by those who greeted me at the door and guided me to a seat, where I was cordially greeted again. It was a climate of expectation. I was ready to discover the environmental view you held of the world where we all live in our common biosphere.

Then something special happened. I looked up and saw the statuette on the altar, with the Master Teacher representing your understanding of who you are in your place in the story. It was a chance for a young environmentalist to see the world through your prism. There stood the Master Teacher on a hillside, talking to people about the world as it was understood in that time. It was in that moment in time that the Teacher began to talk about creating a kingdom of heaven in this biosphere. No, he didn't call it a biosphere. He called earth. We like to call it a biosphere because it makes us acutely aware that we all live in the same world.

In that sculpture on the altar, people were standing and sitting as they listened to what Jesus had to say in his time. Fast-forward to our time, and we can be the ones who are standing and sitting, listening so we can reset our identity for our global age.

What if?

What if, in our time of the tremendous progression of information and knowledge, we are experiencing the obsolescence of an old transcendence view of the world, and the newness of a more humanitarian view for our identity in our digital-information- molecular age? What if that understanding of how to live a successful achievement life can now refocus the dreams and ideals of Jesus into ten words so that, as an update, we hear him speaking anew in our time of The Big Ten Universal Qualities for all mankind? What if these are some of the most important words we can hear now, and what if they are so basic they can be chosen by anyone, anywhere, and anytime as the identity markers we can measure by to be world citizens? And, what if we choose those words to help us reset our identity for our place in the story in our time in history?

In our understanding of our brain through neuroscience, we believe the mind is plastic and can be preset and reset by the identity we input into it. What if the framework for the identity we input to our mind is so basic it doesn't matter whether we are a farmer, mechanic, salesperson, homemaker, or CEO, or whatever ones niche may be, that it doesn't change the Big Ten presets needed to guide a success story? Those ABC's of identity are becoming more and more important in our digital age.

The World Citizen Center echoes the dreams of my granddad and his vision that Big Ten Universal Qualities be taught in all the learning centers of the world to help people define success as chosen qualities of life for a better future. So, what if those ten words fast-forward the teachings of the Master Teacher to us as today's listeners?

What if, in the progression of our science and technology, we find ourselves in the most fantastic Jetson dream cities that technology and engineering have ever built? Well, we are living in that Jetson age of dreams now. We ride in airplanes that fly around our biosphere day after day. We ride in cars that take us to destinations we choose. And we have more and more robots which take digital instructions and then do much of our work for us? You get the idea. Our place in this story would have amazed people only one hundred years earlier. Who are we in this new Jetson age? Are the qualities we measure by keeping up with our science and technology?

What I am proposing is that, if we are wise we will choose those ten qualities which can guide us to a higher humanity, not only in sync with our technology, but with our best dreams. I am saying that we can set a course that aligns today's space ship earth-family so we can dock with an international space station of great dreams for our best tomorrows.

My thesis is that, the way to connect our dreams with great sustainable tomorrows is by teaching the Big Ten Universal Qualities to our children in all kinds of learning centers of the world? That is what will create a healthy environment of the mind in which to define who we are.

What if the world family chooses a framework of identity that so overarches religion, culture, or political persuasion, that we have a knowledge-based faith in which our science, technology and faith connect us together in a new oneness so we can dock with the greatest dreams of all history?

What if religious groupings across the world begin to see the power and potential these ideas can have in helping people put their humanity above their ever changing theological assumptions?

What if, instead of trying to get our beliefs just right, we get our identity markers just right so that we chose those qualities which make our biosphere a wholesome identity environment for our world family?

That is the environment we can create. That is a powerful idea whose time has come! That is where we can work upstream to help build a better people to live in a better Earth biosphere.

When you helped launch the World Citizen Center you were working upstream. Here in this church, when you chose to place a sculpture of the Teacher on the altar of your church to represent a higher vision for the human family, you were working upstream.

Does it make a difference that statuette of the Master Teacher is there before us, representing the quality of our dreams, each time we come here to worship?

I think it does!

Does it make a difference that all of us can update and reframe our guiding markers in the Big Ten Universal Qualities to help us measure for success?

I think it does.

As we learn more about the endless cosmos, there is a sense that our place in the story seems to get smaller and smaller. But, at the same time, the story we are creating here in our biosphere may be getting bigger and more important than ever in comparison to what the story may be on whatever other planets there may be in the cosmos.

What if we discover that the story of the human family's survival against incredible odds across thousands of years, up to our digital-information-molecular age, is truly remarkable?

What if space travelers from another planet were to arrive here and saw our biosphere, would they be impressed by our science and technology, but even more impressed by the Big Ten Universal Qualities as a progression of the identity markers our Earth family is now learning to live by?

What if they chose to take the Big Ten Universal Qualities back to their planet as a model? Does this scenario make us more aware of how important our place in the story in our time in history may be?

Our story is not complete. We are indebted to the past but we owe more to the future.

Our biosphere is our home. It's where we can turn old endings into new beginnings for new tomorrows. It's where the words of the Big Ten Universal Qualities can be chosen as the identity markers we measure by for successful achievement as world citizens. It's where we can be among those who work upstream - where we give our best dreams their best chance to happen in our story.

The yardstick is a universal measure.

The words printed on the Big Ten Yardstick are a universal measure for success.

The words of the Big Ten Universal Qualities are printed in your bulletin in bold type. Reading from the bulletin, or recalling from memory, let us repeat these words together.

KINDNESS, CARING, HONESTY, RESPECT, COLLABORATION, TOLERANCE, FAIRNESS, INTEGRITY, DIPLOMACY, NOBILITY.

It's the new sacred for, new tomorrows and, a place in the story.